A WOLF AMONG MEN

BY EMILY MCCARTNEY NELSON

Copyright ©2024 Line By Lion Publications
www.pixelandpen.studio
ISBN 978-1-948807-24-1
Cover Design by Thomas Lamkin Jr.
Editing by Dani J. Caile

LINE BY LION
PUBLICATIONS

*To all those family and friends along the way who helped
me realize the power of words, and
the importance of following your dreams.*

CHAPTER ONE

A bright sun blazes down over three figures as they stalk slowly across the crumbling remains of a highway overpass. Abandoned cars and trucks don't impede them as the thick blanket of grass and weeds muffles their footfalls. Ivy and other creeping greens cover the last vestiges of concrete and human influence. Above their heads an illegible billboard fades in the sun, its hunter green edges still visible. In front of these three, the crumbling, barely recognizable skyline of Cincinnati still stands as small flocks of birds encircle the collapsed buildings.

The first of the trio stands taller than the others with unevenly cropped auburn hair. Her face holds piercing gray eyes searching the surrounding roadblocks and cars for any sign of movement. Well-toned arms and hands hold a bow and nocked arrow ready in front of her; the left hand grasps the arrow while the right holds the finely made leather grip of the bow. A quiver of arrows hangs off her left hip while a sheathed machete drapes down across her right side. The gray and brown feather in the quiver rustles lightly as she moves across the uneven ground. Despite her lean and powerful body, her heart-shaped face holds the wan, hungry look of one who has gone without food several times in her life.

Walking behind and to her right is another young and shorter woman about the same age. Three long slash scars mar the left half of her face from hairline to chin. Her eyes are mismatched. The left eye stares blankly, its rich brown hue clouded with white. Her tanned skin makes the pale pink of the scars starkly stand out. Dark brown, almost black hair streams down her shoulders to midway down her back, glossy and poker straight. She clutches a crossbow to her left shoulder while its strap wraps across her chest. A long machete on her left thigh matches the one strapped to the leader's right thigh. Even as she steps forward, this raven-haired woman leads with her left foot to keep her right side always facing potential danger.

On the left side of the leader, a man walks proudly with a bow in his arms and a knife strapped on his left hip. Several other daggers hug his calves and an axe sits on the side of the huge pack he wears. Shaggy, brown hair covers his head almost like a mop, with strands and locks framing his bright green eyes on his oval-shaped face. His broad shoulders and well-muscled frame fall three inches short of the leader's six-foot stature, but he easily tops his tracking partner by about four inches.

All three are jumpy as they reach the halfway point across the overpass above the river, and none of them want to get too close to the edge for a peek at the rusting supports or the rushing water beneath.

"Not the best travel day we've had." The man breaks the relative silence between them, adjusting the weight of the heavy pack on his shoulders, so it sits better. "I wouldn't have minded a little cloud cover."

"I'm just glad it's not raining, Charlie," the shorter woman replies, glancing behind them as they continue. "Four days of last week were spent either getting pissed on by the sky or getting thrown around by the river. I don't want to be wet anymore." She shrugs her shoulders in sympathy as her own pack resettles.

Charlie laughs and pokes his partner in the ribs with his right elbow. "We're all tired of the wet, Kiya. I'm just saying I'd be glad of some shade. The sun is burning."

"Keep it down, Charlie," the leader barks. "I don't want to let anything know we're here. I feel too exposed on this bridge. There could be anything on its sides or beneath us. I don't like it."

"Alright, Cleo," Charlie replies as his voice lowers to a whisper. "I'll shush until Elijah finds us a likely spot for the night." He goes back to staring avidly to his left. Kiya on his right keeps her eye roving along their right side. Cleo, in front, keeps her head on a swivel, checking around each vehicle before they pass it. Ahead, another shape gestures at them from a break in a cement wall, making Cleo pause to be certain of what she's seeing.

"Elijah found a way into the city." She lowers her bow and waves at the figure. "I think he'll wait until we're closer before he starts to explore the buildings." The three travelers move on. They occasionally startle the odd sparrow from a weedy bush or chipmunk from the gutted remains of a sedan. Cleo glances up at the bird but judges it too small to be worth the waste of an arrow and doesn't even blink at the retreating rodent. When they move closer to where Elijah waits, a rabbit dashes across the open expanse of weedy concrete. It falls five or six bounds from its starting position with an arrow through its chest. Cleo had barely moved, yet her bow is empty as she moves easily toward her felled prey. Charlie gives a grunt of congratulations and pleasure at the thought of roasting the large animal over a fire for dinner.

"How big?" Kiya moves forward and turns her head a bit so she can see Cleo kneeling beside the furry body to pull the arrow free. "Should we try to down some of the pigeons fluttering near the end of the bridge? I'm sure we could bag a fair few of them."

Cleo manages to rip the arrow from the rabbit's side and pulls the four legs together to tie them deftly with a leather thong from her belt before standing. She ties the thong to the side of her own stuffed pack. "I don't think the pigeons would be worth the arrows and quarrels." At the sight of Kiya's slight frown, she continues, "Not to say we're all bad shots, I just think we could find better game on the ground. Another bunny this size, and we'd be set for a few days with meat." She grins at her friend.

"Maybe we can get a deer once we get out of the city." Charlie looks at the blooming woods around the riverbank and the outskirts of the dead city. "They should be plentiful this time of year. As long as the Lycans haven't been hunting them for lack of anything better to eat." All three faces darken at these words and they all scan around nervously.

"Let's get going," Cleo orders, moving forward again with the rabbit tied to the side of her weighty pack. "I want to be under cover an hour before dark so we can get settled without using torches." And the trio sets off again in the direction of their friend who begins to move into the shade of the buildings.

It takes the three another five minutes before they reach the spot where their friend disappeared. They discover a roughly cut stair-like space leading in between two leaning concrete walls. It seems sturdy enough and Cleo lets her friends go first. She steps back down to street level and waves back the way they came. Almost halfway across the bridge, a lone figure walks half-crouched along the path the three friends just took. To Cleo, the shape isn't distinguishable as man or woman. She knows it is her best friend, Mandi, guarding their rear from attack and making sure they aren't being followed.

We've made it one more day, Cleo thinks as she signals to Mandi. *Let's make it another.* When Mandi waves back a minute or so later, Cleo wipes her hands on her T-shirt and climbs back into the shade to follow her other friends.

*   *   *

Down below the overpass near the bank of the river, two additional human figures pick their way around crumbled concrete chunks and scraps of metal. The front-most figure lifts his head to gaze up at the rusted underbelly of the overpass. Short, dark brown hair covers his peach-fuzzed face. Longer, darker hair covers his head and lays in wavy locks around his face and down his neck. His face is vaguely human in shape, but more elongated and pointed giving him a vulpine look. Ears peek out among the mass of hair; the pinna is pointed at the tips like those of a cartoon fairy. His golden eyes are bright, focused above him. His ears, about an inch further up the head than a human's, perk forward, catching faint snatches of conversation on the wind. He lifts his head up, closing his eyes, and breathes in deeply through his nose, smelling the air. A crease wrinkles his brow and he sniffs again as does his female companion.

"Zoya," he says, his voice is low, almost a growl. "What do you smell?" He doesn't open his eyes but turns his head in her direction.

Zoya's face is even more elongated and narrow than her partner's. The golden fur on her face is a bit thicker than his dark brown mane. A loose-fitting vest of supple animal hide covers her chest to just above her waist where a belted skirt sits snugly on her hips. The exposed skin is covered in the same thick, golden fuzz. A pack is slung across her chest on one shoulder swaying with her movements. Her green eyes close as she inhales deeply, and a similar crease appears on her forehead.

"Four humans, one out further in front, one further back, two grouped together with one other." She glances at him. "The last one, the fifth one smells too … raw … to be human. It's almost a Lycan smell, but it's not enough of either for me to be sure. She's something different."

Themis nods, opening his eyes and glancing northward at the wooded area a few feet from the embankment. "I think we should follow them. Not just for our orders, but to see what exactly she is." The pair pick their way toward the trees, keeping an ear toward the group of humans to be sure they aren't tagged while disappearing into the thick branches.

*   *   *

Once under the cover of the two walls, the temperature drops several degrees to the point where Kiya, in a walking half crouch prepared for anything, is shivering; Charlie can feel her when she accidentally brushes against his bare arm.

"You all right, Kiya?" He gently touches her shoulder.

"Just getting used to the temperature. I was enjoying the sunshine." Her voice grows steadier as she speaks. "Where did Elijah get to?"

"Through here." A different voice drifts down the passage. "There's more open space once you get past the two walls. There's some more sun out here too." The voice is deeper, more of a baritone than tenor, but with a hint of power suggesting the volume could become overpowering at will.

As Charlie and Kiya exit the shadowed hall, brilliant, speckled sunlight dazzles them for a few moments as they gaze around a secluded and well-protected courtyard. Across the clearing, a man kneels, digging in a bag and facing away from the two newcomers.

"I thought this would be a good spot to regroup before we went too much further into the city itself. I know we can cover a little bit more ground today, but I wanted to give Mandi the chance to get caught up before we start hiking through the ruins." The brown-haired man glances up; his darkly tanned skin and growth of stubble down his jaws and chin lend him a warm appearance matching his voice.

"Good idea." Cleo ducks out from under the two-walled tunnel and gazes around the clearing. "Had we come upon this spot later in the day I might have said we should stay here for the night, but I want to get at least another hour's worth of distance under our belts before we stop."

"I know you want to get a bit more distance in tonight, Cleo, but I think this is the best spot to camp." Elijah glances around. "We're sheltered here; we can get some hunting done so we have the meat we need for a good long trek. There is a roadway heading in a roughly northeastern route up toward where we want to go lined by walls and is easy to follow. I climbed one of the walls earlier and there are several roads. It would be a really good way to go for a while, plus a little easier on us."

Cleo glances around at her three companions and hears the rustle of someone coming through the tunnel behind her. "Well, I guess getting the chance to hunt during the day would be nice." She moves aside as the third woman, Mandi, joins the party.

Mandi is almost the same height as Cleo and wears her waist-length hair braided down her back. The overall effect is to give this already strikingly beautiful woman an almost Athena-esque air, however, this effect is marred slightly by a shadow just behind her eyes. Even though her round face glows with an ever-present smile, it doesn't quite travel up to her brown eyes. Her cheeks are flushed from exertion, but her

breath is even as though she had only been on a light stroll on a flat plain.

"I like this spot." Her voice is bright, and her face seems to grow even brighter as she speaks and takes in the dappled splendor of the clearing. "I'll head back out to guard. I want to enjoy the sun for a little while before the shadows get too long."

As if her words had settled everything, Mandi leans her heavy pack against the moss and ivy-covered wall beside her, pulls her quiver onto her back and takes the bow in her left hand back through the concrete tunnel.

With a shake of her head, Cleo raises an eyebrow at Charlie and walks forward and toward the wooded area to the left. "I'm going to go see if I can snag anything before the light runs out. I won't go far."

Charlie turns to Kiya and they begin to pull out tents and sleeping arrangements. With all the packs on the ground in front of them, they begin to sort through the available food supplies, tent materials, bedding and extra socks and sweatshirts they had split between the five of them earlier in the morning.

"Who had the pot?" Charlie asks, rummaging through his own pack in vain. Kiya pulls it from Cleo's pack and sets it behind her.

"Cleo had it today, and I think Mandi had the cups and two of the waterskins if you're thinking about starting a soup." Kiya's voice is patient, running through her mental lists she had made when she packed everyone's bags. "I think we should start carrying the same things in the same packs, just so

things don't get lost or forgotten if we are attacked and don't have time to redistribute everything."

Without another word, she begins her own rummaging and reordering. Charlie leaves her to it, gathering up the pot, cups, and waterskins to start studying the stores to determine what could be managed for dinner. He also grabs the rabbit from Cleo's bag and begins to gut and skin the rodent. His movements are deft as he works, able by this time in his life to skin any animals caught in snares or shot down by arrow or quarrel. He glances at the crossbow by his own pack and grins. He had been the best shot with his crossbow back in their settlement several years ago. He had even won his mom and sister Cleo extra meat servings for the big spring fair when he turned seventeen. Cleo had been so proud of him, standing with their mother, watching him shoot, and cheering when he had hit the bullseye again and again from further and further away. Grinning to himself, Charlie looked down and saw he had finished with the rabbit and set about cutting it up into chunks.

"Do we have any vegetables left?" he asks, turning to Kiya. "I thought we might use some of the potatoes from the garden we were in three days ago. Or what about the carrots? I don't think we used all of those last night."

"I found four or five potatoes here." Kiya holds up a sack in her left hand. "I haven't gotten the carrots yet, but I think we have a good bushel left, provided your sister hasn't been snacking on them earlier today," she smirks. "I know she grabbed one of them as we were walking up to the overpass."

Charlie chuckled. "She said she was hungry. She grabbed one and munched on it, but I don't think she ate more. She prefers fruit when she can get a hold of it. I know she'll be excited when we can find apple trees."

"I'll be excited too," Kiya agrees. "It might actually mean we're safe and getting used to our new homes."

"I hope so." Charlie sighs. "This last year has been really hard on all of us. We deserve a little bit of a break. A little bit of good after everything that's happened." He stands and sets about collecting large stones from the debris surrounding them. When he gets enough to make a decent-sized circle in the center of the clearing, he turns to Kiya.

"Did Elijah go get firewood?" He gazes around the now deserted clearing. "I didn't hear him leave."

"Yeah." Kiya doesn't look up. "You were lost in thought and skinning the rabbit. He said he'd be back with some fresh wood, or he hoped." Kiya looks around. "I finished sorting through most of the stuff. Everything's ready to go except the food stuff and the tents. I do have carrots and potatoes. Do you need more water?"

"We might want to gather some more water while we can." Charlie glances around. "We only have about three skins of water if all were combined. I was thinking about combining them and sending you or Mandi out to get water from the river if we can't find a different source."

"Don't worry about using river water." Elijah walks out of the woods across from the tunnel entrance, laden with wood. "I found a little spring and was planning on grabbing the skins to refill them. I know the two in my bag are close to empty. Try to consolidate water into two or three skins and I'll take the other six or seven with me to the spring."

Charlie crouches with the ten skins and begins the slow process of filling two to bursting and one about halfway. He then ropes the empty eight skins together and hands them to Elijah who takes them easily. "Kiya, do you want to go stay with Mandi while Charlie and I get the water?" Elijah asks gently. "I'm going to need help and I want to make sure you'll be all right for a while."

Kiya scoffs at the concern. "Eli, I'll be fine." Her voice is playful and joking. "I'll get started on the fire and see if maybe I can get the half-skin of water to boil before you both get back." She grabs Charlie's hand and gives it a gentle squeeze. "Just be careful. We need you to help carry the supplies. You're the strongest one aside from me."

Charlie grins before following Elijah into the trees. Among the leaf litter and crumbled building debris, trees and bushes bloom from every side. Wildflowers of every color and size encircle the pair as they trek deeper into the surrounding woods. It takes about two minutes to find the spring and Charlie is glad to find the water is pure, cold, and clear. Elijah kneels beside the pool, burbling slightly with the small gush of the spring, and unties the bundle of waterskins.

Charlie joins his friend on the other side of the pool, leaning down briefly to gulp a few mouthfuls of the fresh water. He dips his hands in the water and runs them across his slightly sunburned face and neck. After the quick ablutions, he helps Elijah fill the seven skins.

It takes close to twenty minutes before they are all full, sealed and distributed between the two men. "We might want to come back here after camp is set up." Elijah says as they stand to head back. "This might be the last place we can all wash in clean water for a while."

On the way, Cleo appears, panting slightly. "I need some help. I managed to find a few more rabbits, but I also brought down a deer. I don't think we can take the whole carcass, but I want to cut off a few decent-sized steaks before the animals get at it." She is bright and flushed with pride at her accomplishment. "I brought it down with one shot." She grins at Charlie and pats the bowstring slung across her chest.

"That's impressive." Charlie grins back. "I'll come help you if Eli can get the water back to Kiya on his own." He looks at his male companion. "What do you think, Eli? Got enough muscle?"

Elijah makes a face at Charlie and grabs the four waterskins slung over his friend's shoulders. He sags a bit under the weight but shrugs. "Not too hard. Bring back as many steaks as you can. Maybe we can find a way to make strips to dry and store them. Bring the skin back too. Any type of animal hide would be helpful for trading or for clothes when we get where we're going."

"Will do, Eli." Cleo grins and reaches out to pat her friend on the shoulder. "We'll be back in a bit." Together, Cleo and Charlie dart off the way Cleo had come.

Not two minutes later, Charlie spots the deer, lying on its side in the mud, an arrow sunk almost to the fletchings in its chest. It was a one-in-a-million shot, not having hit any ribs or anything except a lung and the heart. He whistles low, impressed and a bit jealous of his older sister.

"I couldn't have made the shot," he murmurs, awed. "And I've been working with the crossbow for longer than you've been working with your bow."

"I got lucky." Cleo kneels by the throat of the deer where she begins to work at stripping the skin from the body. Blood, already starting to congeal around the arrow wound, seeps slowly from the cut she makes, but Cleo continues without hesitation. Charlie moves to the animal's belly and makes quick, precise slashes to get a start on removing the animal's bowels before they start poisoning the meat and fouling the area around their work.

After an hour, the two are covered in blood from head to heel, but Cleo grins at her brother. They take the skinned carcass and several steaks of the beast's haunches and sides in their arms, all wrapped in large leaves found from a bush nearby.

"The wolves can have the rest. I think we'll be good on meat for the next couple of days. Especially with the rabbits I've already taken back to camp."

Together, Charlie and Cleo walk back, stopping at the spring to rinse the blood from themselves and their weapons before following the small line of smoke rising into the air. Cleo steps out first, pulls the bow from her shoulders and lays the meat next to Elijah kneeling by the fire.

Charlie follows more slowly, stopping beside Kiya before adding his meat to the pile. The sky by this time is a rosy gold with the shadows growing longer and longer. Elijah breaks off what he's saying and grins at the seven steaks piled on the stone beside him.

"Looks like we'll be set for a while." He peels the leaves off the top-most steak. "I was just saying to the others we should try to get about six hours of walking done tomorrow before we stop to make camp. I'd love to see if we could do eight hours just because we shouldn't need to hunt with all the meat you guys brought back. I'm going to slice the top steak into jerky to eat on the walk tomorrow."

"That sounds like a great idea." Cleo sits down near the fire. "Is Mandi standing guard?" At Kiya's nod, she glances up at the sky. "Charlie, can you and Kiya relieve her? I want to hear what she saw behind us today."

The pair stand and grab weapons before ducking their heads and starting down the tunnel. After they're gone, Elijah looks up at Cleo from his work of making thin strips of the meat and their eyes briefly connect.

"How was scouting today?" Cleo glances to her pack and stands up. "Any problems with the Lycans?"

"I didn't see anything unusual. Just the usual abandoned cars and crumbling structures," Elijah says while he works. "Thought I might have spotted the scat of some real wolves or maybe dogs as I walked toward the bridge but didn't feel the need to track it. It was hard and didn't have any smell to it. It had been out to dry for a while."

"I saw it as I passed too!" Mandi's voice is pleasant and bubbly as she strides through the opening to the concrete space. "I thought about tracking, just to see what I could find, but then I touched it with an arrow, and it rolled away. Didn't think it was worth it."

"But, Mandi, what I'm really asking is did you see anything out of the ordinary?"

"I thought I saw a flicker of movement when I started to cross the bridge." Mandi stares at the fire and the strips of meat laid out on the concrete blocks around the blaze. "I also thought I saw a few figures down by the bank. I leaned over the edge of the overpass to get a look, but they disappeared before I could tell what they were. Probably just a couple of deer or something like the one you shot today."

"Maybe." Cleo's voice is drawn out, hesitant. "I think we should guard the entrance through the buildings tonight. Just to be sure no Lycans find us. It might be a good idea to have someone patrolling this edge of the clearing too." She gestures toward the trees surrounding them. "I'll take first watch by the entrance when it starts to get dark. Eli, is there anything I need to do to the meat as it cooks?"

"Just flip it before you go out to guard," Elijah says, stretching and standing. He slips his knife into a sheath at his right hip and moves toward one of two tents set up with their backs to the crumbling building to the right of the tunnel. "It should be good where it is. Maybe flip it when you come back and by the time we head to bed, the strips may be ready to be bundled. If it's dry to the touch but slightly malleable, it's done."

"Sounds good," Cleo says, nodding to herself. "Mandi, you should get some rest, too. I'll wake you when I go to watch. I'm going to go tell Charlie and Kiya what's going on."

"All right," Mandi replies, moving to the other tent. "I probably won't be asleep, but I'll try to get a bit of rest." Without another word, she ducks beneath the flap.

Out beyond the tunnel, Charlie sits with Kiya, their legs hanging over the edge of the wall of the path they had climbed to reach the clearing. They glance up at the sound of Cleo's soft footfalls.

"We going to take turns guarding?" Kiya asks, glancing around the abandoned landscape. "Front and back? Might be a good idea."

"Yeah." Cleo glances at the bridge they had crossed. "I'll take first watch when night starts to really fall. Mandi will guard the woods and I'll be out here. Charlie, you and Eli will take second watch. Wake me for third watch, and I'll come out of the tent and guard the wood while you're out here, Kiya." Cleo sighs and goes on before either of the others can argue. "I'll take second watch tomorrow night and the four of you can argue about who's going to get up twice on the walk tomorrow." She chuckles and turns to go back to the fire. "I'll come get you two when it's time."

Without another word, Cleo disappears. Not two hours later, she returns with her bow and quiver of arrows in hand. Charlie and Kiya rise and walk back through the tunnel, emerging to see Mandi sitting on a boulder at the far edge of the clearing. With a smile and a nod, she turns to continue gazing at the darkening trees as the pair of them duck into the empty tent to sleep.

CHAPTER TWO

The trees along the large open road flash by with bright budding green and patches of newly blooming yellow flowers; they flourish despite the rot and decay of American civilization. As Cleo scouts almost a mile in front of her group, another figure stalks them, hidden by the brush and branches just over a mile in front of her.

Zoya crouches, watching behind her as she listens for any hint of problems ahead. Her nose is lifted north and eastward, alert for the scent of Lycans nearby. With a glance toward the intersection of two overgrown roads, Zoya heads due north, hoping her quarry will pick the intersecting road following more closely their desired direction. Having overheard some of the conversation in the morning, Zoya knows this group of humans needs to travel north close to where her territory lays, but she isn't sure the best way to approach these people. Zoya knows they are young; their youth is clear just by the way they move and struggle with decisions. She also knows the one they call Cleo is the most knowledgeable and the most able leader.

That's one human I don't want to cross if I can help it. Zoya moves toward an oak standing taller than the other maples and birches nearby. She grabs the lowest branch and is halfway up and glancing furtively over the lower treetops in time to catch a glance of Cleo as she approaches the intersecting paths at a trot. Her subject glances down the intersection, and then forward along the road she is currently on before kneeling and rummaging in the ground. Zoya tilts her head to the side but climbs down as Cleo starts moving along the path.

Just as I thought. Zoya follows the group just beside the chosen road. She stays out of sight as much as possible, trotting through abandoned and collapsed houses and other buildings without much thought to where she is going. She keeps her ears perked and her nose up for any scent of Omegas in the area.

Just a few days ago, Omegas had been seen in greater numbers. She knows one pack enjoys traipsing along the riverbank well ahead or well behind the local Alphas and Betas patrolling the area for the Chicago Territory on a regular basis. She is sure at some point a pack of Omegas will descend on this small band of humans and when it happens she doesn't know who will likely survive. Probably Cleo and maybe her brother Charlie.

In a sudden dash of shadow and rustle of bracken, a man trots through the brush toward Zoya; his face is more elongated than hers with more pointed ears and strangely proportioned arms and legs. The fur covering his body is thick and matches the silvery gray on the top of his head, but Zoya knows this marks the color of his coat rather than his age.

"Miss Zoya." The words are strongly flavored with the sounds of growls and yips. The man speaks with the inflection of a Delta who wasn't educated on how to speak like a human. "I've come from our Alpha. He wants me to check on the progress of your mission."

Of course. Zoya rolls her eyes. *Our fearless leader wants to know how we're coming on the "Human Project."* She sighs and looks down at this smaller Delta, whom she outranks.

"We've found a small band of humans," Zoya snaps, motioning in their direction like she's willing them to continue moving north just on the edge of the road. "We're seeing if they will lead us to a bigger group of them. We think there's going to be a large settlement further north. We're trying to help this group get through most of the small bands of Omegas. Their leader is less than a mile away, and I want to stay well ahead of her."

"Where is Themis?" the messenger asks, glancing around. "I was told you were his Beta during this expedition. Shouldn't he be with you?"

"My Alpha is currently guarding the band's eastern flank and rear. You will probably find him just a few miles down the large road this smaller one intersects." Zoya points him in the general direction where she can sense her Alpha. Having worked with Themis for several years before, she has learned to sense just where he is from the faint scents and pull of his mental control. She had become accustomed how Themis liked his missions to run and how she must keep track of her slightly wayward leader.

"Listen to me: I would strongly recommend you allow the leader to pass and give her a good head start before you go anywhere near their line of walking. They have proven at least two, if not more of them, are well-trained with the bows and crossbows they carry."

"Well understood." The messenger falls back as Zoya moves on at a trot. Ahead, the sign of a recent pack of Omegas is obvious to anyone. The remaining building's walls are covered in scratch marks and the ground is littered with dried blood, scat, bones, and scraps of cloth. The rank reek of unwashed bodies mixes foully with rotting flesh.

Disgusting. Zoya wrinkles her nose and eases her way across the patch of carnage. *At least it looks like only two or three. There would have been a lot more blood and bones had it been a larger pack. They would have taken down any living thing instead of just hunting a human.*

Zoya glances around, looking for the Omegas' trail and finds it almost immediately. Two distinctly different scents alert her to the suspicion of a smaller pack traveling east, but in the western corner, she catches the scent of a third participant in this pack. The howling comes from just north of where she stands, and Zoya is aware the group is moving toward the lone human who approaches them.

I wish they'd use their whole brain. Zoya runs toward the sounds of the howls. *Cleo doesn't even smell fully human. They just know she'll fill their bellies like other meat won't. The partial human scent is enough to drive them crazy.*

Before she gets more than a few dozen paces from the bloody clearing, she spots the outlines of the blood-crazed Omegas.

From her semi-hidden spot, Zoya can see their wolfish shapes distinctly. Their skulls have a much longer and pointed snout with much thicker fur all over their bodies than hers and Themis, matted with blood, gore, and mud. Ragged strips of animal skins hang from their hips, mostly covering them, but their movements are jerky and excited, so the modesty gained by the scraps is minimal at best. Their arms almost brush the ground with long, powerful fingers and sharp claws. The shoulders and necks are strong and thick with muscle, reinforced to better attack and take down prey. Their legs are shorter, stockier, and look almost like the hind legs of wolves with huge thigh, calf, and hamstring muscles. They move with ape-like loping strides that carry the scraggly creatures at an impressively quick pace.

Before they can ambush the humans, Zoya steps out into their path and howls to get their attention from their blood-crazed frenzy. They turn to her with dazed, stupid eyes. Despite this, they hold a small bit of low cunning and one of the three starts to stalk off toward Zoya's left side. She snarls a warning as if to say, "I see you, and you can't corner me."

In a string of yaps and growls, the leader of the pack steps forward. *"What are you doing here, Lieutenant?"*

"I'm following orders from my Alpha," Zoya replies in the same way, snapping and snarling. Sensing a coming brawl, she begins to let the wolf side of her be free. She feels her limbs strengthening, claws growing and sharpening; her face snarls with a much more pronounced wolfish snout. *"These humans are under the protection of the Chicago Territory."*

"We don't care about your territory." The leader hunches forward and the other two pounce with unerring grace and power toward Zoya. After this announcement, their snarls and yelps are only met with pain.

The two followers go for Zoya's forelegs while the leader lunges for her throat. Despite being three on one, Zoya has had years of experience battling Omegas both in play and for her life. She darts forward, avoiding the two going for her legs, taking the leader head on. She ducks her head and charges, taking a slight nip to her neck before ripping at the challenger's belly with her long claws. The piteous whine renders a pause from the other two, giving Zoya the chance to throw the Omega who sliced her to the ground and attack the Omega on her left. The challenger on the right, sensing a much stronger foe than he was expecting, tucks in his matted tail and runs, abandoning his friends to their fate.

The special human can handle one scared Omega. The one she scratched lays curled on her side, not moving except to pant and whine. Zoya now circles the other Omega who growls and snarls more for effect than communication. Zoya ignores the bluff and lets herself bristle and grow as large as she can.

As a Beta, Zoya could be extremely intimidating to any foes she faces. When in her wolf form, her snout and proportions mirror the Omegas in front of her, but she stands usually about five feet and nine inches tall while these in-bred cousins and flea-bitten savages only reach five feet tall. Her caramel-colored fur, when fully bristled and raised, adds another two to four inches to her bulk and intimidation.

"You don't scare me," she hisses, spittle flying out. *"I think you're pathetic, and not worth the effort."* Then he flies at her, his black fur bristled but matted and unkempt. His attack is sloppy, and she manages to duck his jump and rake his forelegs in passing. Without missing a beat, she sweeps a claw

into his throat and it gushes like plump fruit. When her teeth sink into the blood-matted fur and into the soft flesh beneath it, he whines in fear. Without hesitating, she jerks her head sideways and feels the bones of his neck snap and his windpipe crumble beneath her strong jaws.

The last injured Omega finally struggles to her feet and flees, dripping blood as she heads west in a sheer rush to get away from the Beta who destroyed her pack. Zoya has no worries about leaving her in her injured state. There is no way this Omega can last longer than a few hours judging by where Zoya's claws raked her. There is little chance her guts haven't been pierced. Zoya has known one of her Deltas to have suffered a similar wound only to die an hour later from blood loss.

With a sigh of relief, Zoya regains her more human appearance and drags the dead Omega further away from the road she knows Cleo will soon be surveying. Zoya hopes she will run into the injured Omega, kill it and plan to take her little band a few more miles before they rest. *After all, she's a smart girl and must know the smell of blood will draw other hunters and scavengers.*

Zoya and Themis, who had found the deer not ten minutes after Cleo and Charlie had left it, had cut several steaks from its hide before hurrying away to let the dogs have their feast. Zoya realized the taste of deer flesh hadn't been nearly as bad as she thought. Lycans may soon need to rely on more than just consuming humans soon, as the smaller settlements were being raided and the larger settlements more strongly fortified. Some of the city settlements are even making much more deadly weapons like guns and cannons which have the ability to poison Lycans if shot. It wasn't the first time she had had to eat a herbivore to keep from starving. But other Lycans who had never been out of the territory had never eaten the meat of other beasts. They didn't know any other way than how they'd been raised: eating humans every few days to keep themselves fed and strong.

I wonder if the Roaming Alphas left the territories because they wanted another way to live. She glances around and climbs into a thick-trunked maple tree to wait, her thoughts on the humans and her seemingly fruitless mission.

*   *   *

The whining and piteous cries reach Cleo through the trees, so she stands ready when a figure approaches, loping through the brush. She looses an arrow at the shape and in one smooth motion pulls a second from the quiver at her hip, nocks it, draws, and looses it again almost in one breath. The whines get louder and at the impact of the second arrow, there is a yelp followed by a growl. Almost directly in front of Cleo, the threatening shadow she wounded coalesces into the form of a snarling Omega with two arrows in its right side.

Cleo pulls a third arrow from the quiver and has it nocked and drawn as the creature gains ground. She darts left, leaping from a large boulder of debris and while loosing the arrow from the air, hits the creature in the middle of its back. She lands and rolls sideways as the Omega searches in a frenzy to find her and the source of its pain. Cleo lashes out with her bow in her right hand; her left braced like the second hand on a great sword's hilt to balance the swing. The wood cracks the snout of the Lycan, who turns its head away, giving Cleo a few seconds to pull her machete from her belt with her left hand.

As the wolfish creature leaps at her, she ducks and steps forward, raising the blade. With a satisfying jerk of her wrist, the machete catches the Lycan just below its breastbone and slices it from sternum to groin. It drops and rolls away from Cleo as she raises herself from the dusty ground, wiping blood from her eyes.

The Lycan shudders once and then expires as Cleo feels her chest heaving with effort and hands shaking from the surge of adrenaline to her system. She kneels to wipe the blood off her blade on the thick coat of the Lycan before stowing it, raising her left hand to her lips and letting loose a long, shrill whistle which cuts through the still cool spring air. When her whistle fades, she waits a second before hearing the answering whistle. A few seconds later, an even fainter whistle answers the second.

Cleo sighs and rolls her head on her neck to stretch the sudden tension from her muscles while reaching down and pulling out her arrows from the Lycan's body. She wipes them on the matted pelt before stowing them in her quiver once again. As she resettles herself, the emotions from the fight crash over her and pulse hard through her frame.

It takes her friends just under five minutes to arrive. Elijah, Kiya and Mandi almost skid to a stop when they catch sight of the monster lying dead across the road.

"What happened?" Elijah bursts out, walking toward the shaking frame of their leader. "Are you okay? Did you get bitten? What's going on?"

The barrage of questions makes Cleo smile weakly as she turns to her friends. "I'm fine," she replies, raising a hand to the approaching Elijah. "I wasn't bitten. It hardly got near me. I feathered it three times before it tried to get at my throat. I sliced it open. I'll be fine in a minute. I just need to get myself to calm down." Her voice is steady despite her shivering and Elijah nods, glancing at the other two.

"Was it just one?" Mandi asks, stepping toward the filthy body. "They usually travel in packs. Are you sure there aren't any others?"

"I heard a bunch of growling and howling about seven minutes before this one showed up, running like it had the devil on his heels," Cleo responds, repulsed by the stinking creature. "I thought there might have been a fight within the pack. Maybe the others are too wounded or dead. This one was the coward and fled."

Kiya shrugged, moving toward Cleo and Elijah, leaving Mandi the closest to the dead Lycan. "I'd rather not wait around to find out if its buddies are just waiting around for him to come back or to attack while our guard's down."

"Mandi, Eli, go set up a perimeter to ensure we're safe while we wait for Charlie to catch up," Cleo orders, glancing around. "Kiya, keep your crossbow out and ready. I'll be on the lookout as well. I'll signal when Charlie gets here so we can move out again. I think we'll stay closer together for the rest of today's journey. We've only been on the road about two hours. We need to get in another four or so today."

With a nod, the other three go about their assigned tasks and Cleo re-nocks an arrow to her bow. Despite the hit from earlier, the stout oak of the double curved bow seems unaffected by its jarring use as a bat; it has only a small nick in the side from a tooth or claw in the fight. Cleo brushes her finger along the new imperfection, smiling grimly at the additional scar to the wood she had used for almost two years. It takes Charlie only another five minutes to reach Cleo and Kiya. He inches up so quietly that when he pops into their clearing Kiya swings wildly around and nearly pulls the trigger of her crossbow before realizing it's her friend.

"Jeez-us, Charlie!" Kiya shouts, nearly throwing her crossbow to the ground. "I nearly shot you!" She turns to Cleo. "God, this idiot wants to die!"

Cleo chuckles at Kiya's frustration and adrenaline-fueled anger before giving her brother a situation update. "I'm not hurt, nor are the others, but we aren't sure if there are others in the area or not. I want to get going as soon as possible." With that, she lifts two fingers to her lips and gives out two short whistles.

Within two minutes of the sound, two sets of footsteps precede the arrival of Mandi and Elijah. Each one gives Charlie a cordial greeting before they look to Cleo for confirmation.

"We saw nothing, but we only went a few yards around where you guys were standing," Mandi reports as the band of five get into a loose formation with Cleo in front, followed by Elijah, Mandi and Kiya, and Charlie behind everyone.

"Hopefully, we can keep anything else crossing our path simply by being more numerous than the other party."

"I didn't see anything really concrete while I was scouting," Charlie pipes up from the back as Cleo starts moving. "There was a shadow following me for a bit, but it went away. I think it might have just been a dog. I sent a quarrel at it, just to discourage it, but I don't think I hit anything, and it disappeared pretty quickly."

Cleo hesitates but continues on, giving a surreptitious glance behind them. She steps forward and they begin their trek. Not half a mile from where they started, the smell of fresh blood reeks from the bushes to the right and Cleo turns with her nose wrinkled in distaste.

Pushing aside the low branches, Cleo jumps back in surprise and horror. The branches, now drawn aside, reveal the second body of a Lycan, lying in a pool of its own blood. It stirs feebly in response to the sound Cleo makes, and moves its head in their direction.

"What should we do?" Kiya asks. "It looks like it got in a fight. I don't think it could hurt us if it tried."

As if in response, the Lycan struggles to get to its feet, but when it lurches forward, its stomach tears and a gush of intestines falls out. Its breathing is torturous, uneven, and barely perceptible except when it gasps for as much air as it can. With another groan and death twitches, it falls over, its eyes rolling back in its head.

Without thinking, Cleo pulls her machete and steps forward, plunging the blade into the creature's heart and giving it a sharp twist. The body beneath her jerks once and then lays still. Cleo yanks the blade up, wipes it on the fur of the dead creature, and returns to the road. A single tear glistens on her cheek for the briefest of moments before she scrubs it away with the back of her left hand in the same movement as she replaces her machete at her belt.

"Let's go." She walks forward and her friends follow her.

*   *   *

As the first of the shrill whistles cut through the air further north of his position, Themis catches the scent of the Delta headed his way. He rolls his eyes, recognizing the scent of the messenger as one of the lackeys he had worked with when he was training for this mission. Alphas must recognize those who are bringing messages to ensure false information from other territories don't get mixed up with the Alphas' information. Each territory was protective of its resources and didn't want other groups knowing what they were planning. As the Delta approaches, a second whistle breaks through the air. Themis sighs. *Something has happened and now the humans are all in a bit of a panic.* This didn't bode well for being able to keep an eye on them. The Delta catches Themis as he trots several yards behind the last human; the woods beside the abandoned road seem easy to travel through.

"*Themis.*" The Delta's growl is formal and low pitched. He bows his head and then runs up to keep even with Themis's stride. "*I come from Chicago. The Wise Alphas would like a report on what you have found. I spoke to Zoya, but she didn't give me any detailed information."*

"Well." Themis's tone is short; his focus is on his quarry. *"I would love to give you some more information, but I want to see what has these humans all riled up."* The pair of them lope along until Themis spies the man they call Charlie stop moving and glance at the ground in front of him. He seems to chuckle to himself and turns left to a side road up an intersecting road. After about a minute, Themis steps out onto the main road to see where and why Charlie stopped. A line of pebbles is arranged in the shape of an arrow pointing toward the side road. Themis smiles at the clever ways the humans communicate while they are spread out.

The two Lycans trot ahead, following Charlie as he moves toward the whistles of his companions. Not half a mile away, Zoya catches up to them. Themis immediately smells Lycan blood mixed with stale human blood. Zoya's animal skins and her own skin are spattered by droplets of fresher blood.

"Omegas, three of them," Zoya says, eyes steady on Themis's worried face. "I killed one, wounded another, and I think our friends killed the third. He ran off before I could get him." She turns to the messenger. "Looks like he found you."

"He did." Themis rolls his eyes. "Didn't have the chance to ask me questions. Charlie started jogging when he heard the whistles." He turns to the messenger. "We are on the tail of a group of five humans. We believe they are moving up toward the Northern Settlement. There haven't been any other humans this way in the last several weeks since we've been on patrol. We were planning on following these five up north to see the state of the settlement to determine if there is any hope of storming the place or at least picking off the farming humans a few at a time. Any other questions?"

"Yes." The messenger cocks his head. "Why are you protecting these humans? What are they to you? Why don't you just herd them toward the Chicago Territory and be done with it?"

Themis rolls his eyes again. "Because I don't feel five humans would be a good enough supply of bodies for the territory's food supply. I think if we can get a good look at the set-up of the Northern Settlement we might be able to swarm it and integrate the whole population into the Chicago Territory's food supply." His voice becomes a low growl. "I don't appreciate a Delta coming down from the Wise Alphas to tell me I'm not doing my job correctly. I rank just as high as they do. Maybe even higher since I was born of two of the first Alphas in the territory. I can decide how I run my mission."

The messenger takes a hesitant step backwards, bows, and turns to go. Without watching him leave, Themis and Zoya turn to follow their little band of humans further north. As they move to catch up, Themis catches a scent on the wind.

"There's another Alpha tracking us," he mutters to Zoya. "He's too far for me to get a good idea of where he is, but he's definitely following us." With effort, he refocuses his attention on the five and pinpoints they are more to the northwest of him now.

"Do you want to take point for a while?" Zoya asks, watching him focus. "You might have better luck handling any Omegas we come across."

"Yes," he replies. "I might be able to get a closer sniff at our hiding friend while I'm at it. But I'll try and keep the Omegas out of the humans' way as much as I can."

His loping stride is easy, unhurried. He knows he can get in front of the humans in about five minutes of straight running, so he takes a little bit of a loop to get an idea of the surrounding area before taking the point position about a mile in front of Cleo. He gets a better scent of the Alpha stalking the party of five, and knows he is older, not quite as old as the Wise Alphas who are trying to control his mission, but not quite as young as himself. He has heard of Roaming Alphas before but hadn't thought they were anything more than a myth told to young Lycans to keep them from misbehaving.

I don't know how he can survive without a pack. Depending on where packs of Omegas have settled, there is usually about five to ten miles between "territory" lines where the different packs prowl. Themis wants to make sure they are at least four miles free from Omegas before he would even consider letting down his guard. *I couldn't imagine living with only myself. I like being just with Zoya, which is why I took this mission, but to be alone would be unbearable.*

He glances up, a whiff of dog in his nose and grimaces. *Not dog again!* He sighs and goes in search of the prey, hoping against hope it is just one dog and not a pack of them. He can handle one or two, but more than two and he'll be scratched and bloody for days—he has no desire to fight more for his supper. Eating dog was bad enough but having to fight them was just undesirable to the extreme and he didn't relish the thought of bringing Zoya dog meat again. The look on her face when he did it the first time screamed of absolute loathing.

Themis sets his shoulders and darts off, keeping his ears and nose tuned to what Cleo and the others are doing as well as having an awareness of any other Lycans in the vicinity. His mind lingers on the stalking Alpha waiting in the wings as well, wondering if he could be persuaded to join them, or at least to reveal himself as friend or foe to better establish their relationship. So far, he had stayed too far away to be heard by Zoya or Themis, but his scent keeps catching in the air, making both pause in their pursuit of the humans.

When Themis reaches the spot where the scent of dog is strongest, he finds only three dogs ravaging the carcass of a small faun caught wandering in the wooded area. Only one of the dogs has caught wind of him as he steps within their small feeding area and now growls to alert its companions. The first dog is a light gray, almost white if it has been cleaned and well-kept as a pet. Its fur is longer, matted with blood and mud, the teeth it bares are sharp, strong, and set in well-muscled jaws. The other two canines are mixes of black, brown, and a russet brown like the rusting iron of bridges. None of the animals comes up past about mid-thigh on Themis. He briefly snorts before focusing on his task, allowing himself the luxury of transformation so he doesn't bother with a knife. He continues to feel uneasy using his powers despite the years of training. Nothing compares to being able to attack something with your own hands and, in his case, claws.

Themis growls at the challenge from the lead dog, the gray one, his own snout elongating as his shoulders broaden and his arms lengthen, leaving him leaning forward on his newly clawed hands, his powerful back legs hunched and ready. The lead dog pants quickly and takes a small step backwards before snarling in response to his growling challenge. He charges.

The other two hesitate and Themis is grateful for this hesitation as it takes him a few minutes to tackle the lead dog. While the animal isn't particularly large, it is far more clever than Themis had originally thought. Before Themis has his opponent on the ground, the second and third dog leap for him. With a quick slash at the lead dog's throat to keep it from moving too far, he turns to face the new threats. These two are less intelligent than the first, but they are slightly larger using more brute force. Themis uses claws more than teeth against the two dogs, more from wanting to save his energy than inability. Soon the first dog lies dead, but the other two are still alive trying to slink away on broken limbs or with scraped and slashed sides. It takes seconds before they are both dead with broken necks and Themis stands, slowly transforming back to his human shape.

Dinner. Themis considers the three lean, boney shapes before him. *Not much to look at, but maybe it will be better than it looks.* Without another thought he pulls a knife from his belt and begins skinning the beasts.

CHAPTER THREE

Mandi suppresses a yawn into the back of her left hand as she wanders the broken-down and overgrown houses and streets, trying to find a good spot to camp. It has been a long day, starting with quite a surprise. Mandi knew going on this journey would be dangerous, but to encounter the remains of an Omega after it had attempted to kill Cleo, as well as another one dying of wounds from something else, had finally driven home just how daunting their task was.

I guess life or death didn't really take hold in my mind until I saw the death part. Mandi pushes away a thick bramble branch as she gazes around, looking for a nice flat area for them to set up camp. Nothing around here is a strong candidate. As she turns to explore the ruins of a two-story house, she hears Cleo's voice calling their names. Mandi turns and follows the call, walking up to what remains of a church according to the still legible sign. The building is collapsed but seems to be a good open place well surrounded by walls suitable for a campsite.

"Charlie found the spot," Cleo explains as Mandi walks forward. "The entrance to the open space is just around the corner of this close wall." She points and Mandi follows where she indicates.

She follows the curved wall around the remains of the building, and when the corner falls away to reveal an opening,

Mandi squeezes through the gap and into a more field-like area. Ahead, Charlie kneels on the ground, glancing around for stones to set up a fire pit. Mandi kneels at the entrance to the building and picks up several large stones to bring them to Charlie. He glances up, barely registering who it is before grabbing the stones and placing them in the large circle.

"Thanks." His mutter is distracted, and Mandi leaves him to his thoughts. She can't help wondering if it is really worth it to go all the way up to the Northern Settlement. They kept finding nice, well-sheltered areas to hide out and camp for the night. Wouldn't it make more sense to settle in one of these spots, keep out of the way of the Lycans all together and just disappear into the wilderness? Or better yet, couldn't they go back to their old settlement? When they left the Tennessee Settlement, there was an understanding about how safety couldn't be ensured, but what if the situation has changed? What if there was better protection now? They could go back to see. And if it still wasn't safe, they could just continue further south. There wouldn't be any snow or problems if they went down to the Florida Settlement. Mandi didn't understand why Cleo had chosen to go north instead of south.

"Need some wood, Charlie?" Elijah's voice breaks Mandi's thoughts to pieces and she glances up to see Elijah walking in with an armload of branches and sticks. "I found this while I was searching for a spot. You found a good one, though. I'm impressed with how most of the walls are still a decent height considering how large the building was originally. We were lucky today."

"Thanks, Eli." Charlie's tone is a little lighter than it was when he thanked Mandi for the stones, but there is still an edge of irritation and inner turmoil. "Just finished the fire pit. I was about to head out for some wood. Do you still have any of the venison steaks from yesterday? I ate a few of my jerky slices but could do with some freshly cooked meat tonight."

"I was thinking the same thing." Elijah lays down the wood near the fire pit, shrugging the bag off his shoulders. "I think I still have about five steaks left wrapped in the deer hide. I can cook one up and we can share it for dinner. I want to see if I can make some more of the jerky slices tonight too just so we can have those for a while."

And with that, everyone unpacks. Mandi can hear Cleo, still outside the walls, keeping an eye on the entrance and Kiya stalking beside her. Mandi shrugs off her own pack, lays it beside Elijah and then retrieves Cleo and Kiya's packs.

The two girls are standing outside the entrance to their hidden haven when Mandi pops her head out and they both glance her way. Cleo is covered in spattered and dry blood from the Lycan she had killed earlier. Kiya has a look of sympathetic agitation and worry on her own face, mirroring Mandi's own worries.

"The boys are unpacking," she tells her friends, glancing between them. "Charlie's getting a fire set and Elijah's going to cook some of the venison for dinner. What would you like for the three of us to do? Or do you want to try and get yourself washed off? Do you want me to scout around the church at all?"

"I think we should all settle down and get everything prepared." Cleo's voice is just as clipped as her brother's had been. "I'll scout and see if I can find a creek for water. I think we just need one guard tonight, so the watches will be shorter, and everyone will get the chance to have a longer sleep. But I want us all to be ready to leave at a moment's notice. I don't like how close we came to an attack today. I want us to get as far from here as we can tomorrow morning. I remember hearing how Lycans had taken over most of the area around this abandoned city, but I didn't think it was bad. Now I'm thinking we might have been wiser to go around the city."

"I agree." Kiya nods and reaches out her hand. "Give me your pack. We'll get everything settled and then one of us will come and relieve you before nightfall."

Cleo shakes her head, looking at the entrance. "No, I want to talk to you guys before we settle into the routine of getting ready for bed." The three girls go and join the boys sitting around the fire.

Charlie glances up and is standing over his small blazing fire in an instant after looking at his sister's face. "Cleo, what's wrong?"

"I'm all right, just a bit tired." Cleo waves her brother back to what he is doing. "I did want to see how everyone was feeling and see if anyone had any grievances with our plan to go north."

Now's your chance, a little voice in Mandi's head says. *Tell her what you think. Ask her why we should be going north instead of south.* Mandi bites her lip and takes a deep breath.

"Why didn't we go south when we left our settlement?" she demands, looking at Cleo with a blazing stare. Cleo turns and stares right back at her. "Why did we go north? If we had gone south, we wouldn't be worried about weather or other problems like it getting cold in winter. I don't see why we went north. It doesn't make sense. At least, not to me."

Cleo's gaze is hard, evenly matched with Mandi's. A little part of Mandi almost immediately wants to curl up and forget she had spoken, but she keeps herself together.

"We went north because it was the best chance for survival," Cleo responds, her tone solid and defensive. "Yes, we will have to deal with cold and snow and ice come winter, but we will learn to deal with it just like we've learned to deal with other things. We went north because the settlement up north is the strongest of the human settlements left on this continent. Had we moved south, we would have run the risk of taking a wrong turn into the southern Lycan territory and I didn't want to risk it. I have walked some of the route to the Northern Settlement with my mother when I was little, so the route is a little bit more familiar to me than the route south." Cleo's eyes blaze again as if challenging Mandi to speak again.

"I think once we get away from the city and closer to the settlement, we should be safe. We just have to get there." Charlie adds his gaze to Mandi's. "Today was rough, but it was also the first time we've run into any Lycans since the attack on our settlement. I think we should take it as a blessing. We could have been hounded all the way here."

"Good point, Charlie," Kiya adds her voice. "I don't like the thought of facing any more of the beasts myself, but I think this is the best way we could have come, all things considered."

Mandi sighs and breaks eye contact with Cleo and turns to Elijah sitting across from Charlie at the fire side. "What about you, Eli?"

Elijah takes a few minutes to compose himself. "I don't like the thought of having to travel through more Lycan-infested woods, but I will say, I am glad we haven't run into more Lycans from the beginning of the journey." He glances at Cleo, his eyes soft and kind. "I know Cleo has been doing as much as she can to keep us all together and to keep us safe. I think we should continue, despite the danger. I did want to know the reasoning behind the decision to go north, but now you've shared, it makes sense to me and I don't have a problem with the decision. It was a good one considering all the problems with both choices."

Cleo smiles for the first time since they decided on campsites. "Well, then I'm going to go back out. Come get me when night falls." She shoulders her quiver and moves along the exit of the building's walls.

"I still don't like having to continue on," Mandi grumbles, kneeling by her bag to grab one of the waterskins she carries.

Charlie glances up at her and huffs. "Well, then I'm sorry it's not your decision." His voice is testy. "You are more than welcome to go back the way we came and see if you can get back past other Lycans that might have moved in since we killed the two in the city earlier." His tone is dark, almost laughing at her. "Or, you can just shut your trap and we can get to safety in a few days and we'll be fine."

Mandi glares at him, then focuses on pulling and laying out her sleeping roll as far from Charlie as she can get without sacrificing the warmth of the fire.

Kiya takes her portion of venison and eats it quickly, keeping an eye on the sun as it sinks lower. "I'll go relieve Cleo in a little bit. Then she can enjoy some warm food and a bit of a nap. Is everyone packed and ready to go tomorrow morning?"

"As long as you turn the jerky once when you come back from your guard and whoever guards after you dampens the fire, we should be good to go." Elijah looks over his stones covered by jerky slices. "I have two more steaks wrapped in the deer hide. I think I'll strip those tomorrow and then we'll just try to live on jerky and soups the rest of the trip."

"Sounds like a plan." Kiya smiles at him. She sighs contentedly as she gobbles the rest of the meat. By the time the rest of the meat is finished cooking a few minutes later, she heads out to begin her watch.

Mandi sulkily accepts her piece of meat and munches gloomily as she glares at Cleo entering the campsite. Cleo doesn't look at her, ignoring the daggers shooting from Mandi's eyes, and sits beside Elijah to take her chunk of meat and lay her head on his shoulder. Mandi grunts in the back of her throat before turning away and finishing her meat. It doesn't take long before she is rolled in her sleeping bag and snoozing away.

*   *   *

Zoya's legs ache from the rushed pace the humans keep during the day. She can tell the attack from the Omega has spooked them. While they usually travel more spread out with one scouting far ahead, three in the middle and one guarding their rear, after the fight they stayed in a tight formation with Cleo in the lead only scouting a few yards ahead at a time. They are more alert to everything going on around them now. If they keep the same formation for the rest of the trip, it'll make tailing them a little bit easier. But at the same time, if they keep their current pace, they'll certainly be exhausted by the time the fourth day arrives. "You ready to switch places?" Themis's voice vibrates from just behind her and she jumps at its suddenness. "Sorry, I thought you had heard me coming. I wasn't being sneaky this time."

"You're fine." Zoya chuckles lightly at her own foolishness. "I was just distracted by my thoughts. Do you think the humans will keep the same pace they did today? I hope they don't tire themselves out too quickly."

"They might keep it up tomorrow, just to get out of the city limits and away from the worst of the Omega packs, but they'll probably slow down again when they get out more into open territory. They'll have to be more aware of their surroundings once they're in the old farm territory. There are fewer trees and forests to hide them."

Zoya nods and sighs. "What did you find out from your spying and eavesdropping? Nothing too embarrassing for anyone, was it?" Her joke makes Themis smile as he starts to tell what he had heard from the humans around their camp.

"One of the girls wishes they had gone south from their home settlement, but she's the only one willing to turn back." Themis's smile turns grim. "I'm worried she might do something stupid to get her friends to go back to where she feels safe. But everyone else is set on continuing north to the settlement up there. I think they called it the Northern Settlement. Apparently, the leader has been part of the way there before. She thinks they will be safe there, they just need to get away from this city. Did you find any sign of Omegas at all?"

"Nothing," Zoya responds, scrubbing at one of her eyes. "Which is good and bad, wouldn't you say? I would have expected to have found at least some sign of the mutts around here even if it was just old scat, but there isn't anything. So, either there haven't been any packs around here, or the bastards are getting cleverer and can make it seem like they haven't been somewhere."

"I'll take a look for a while," he says. "Go lie down and get a bit of rest. I'll come find you to take turns keeping watch for the night when I've scouted a few miles around the area."

"Sounds good." Zoya yawns and turns to head toward the humans' camp. "I'll go find a spot to see if I can hear any more from the human quarter." She walks away, stretching and preparing to lie down for a while.

She reaches the small patch of woods just out of sight of the walls the humans had chosen to shelter behind. The leader paces around the entrance to their campsite, her bow nocked with an arrow in her hands. Zoya sniffs, checking the camp's security while noticing the faint smell of the strange Alpha still sitting at the knife edges of being able to sense him. She couldn't get more of the scent than just he was an Alpha and he was following them.

We should try to talk to this Alpha. Maybe he could help us keep an eye on this little band of humans. Maybe he's just another one of the Alphas from the Chicago Territory just trying to keep an eye on any prime human candidates for the food supply in the territory.

She lays on her stomach, her chin pillowed by her crossed forearms as she gazes fixedly on the group. The muffled sound of words comes to her from the leader and Zoya focuses to hear better.

"It's not like I didn't ask for them to question me," Cleo grumbles to herself. "But I guess I didn't realize just how strongly Mandi feels about this desperate trip. Well, if she feels so strongly about her idea to go back south, she's more than welcome to go herself. I won't stop her." The fuming dies to a slow grumble coming from the girl's chest. Her pacing is angry and irritated.

Zoya chuckles silently to herself. *There must be trouble in paradise. I wonder how long this one is going to be able to keep her calm with her friends. It sounds like one of them started questioning her. She doesn't seem to like it. She sounds like Themis when I don't do what I'm supposed to.* The thought makes Zoya glance about to ensure her Alpha isn't in the immediate vicinity. When assured she is alone, Zoya sighs and settles in to watch.

It takes Themis about forty minutes to get back to where Zoya lays, keeping an ear out for any incoming threats. She glances up at her leader and smirks.

"Nothing around? Hmmm. Maybe we should consider taking tonight as a chance to get to know our secret stalking neighbor. I can still smell him, but I can't get anything concrete."

"I was thinking about it as I was traveling back here." He had come from just south of the humans' camp and Zoya wonders if he too had tried to follow the Alpha's scent. "I don't think he'll let me get close to him, though. I think he knows I'm another Alpha and doesn't want to risk getting caught up in a fight with me. Maybe he'll let you get closer as an envoy."

"Sure, I'll go." Zoya stretches from her comfortable spot on the ground and pushes herself to her knees. She pulls at the belt around her waist which holds a variety of small knives and dislodges it. "Probably a better idea for me to go to him as unarmed as possible. I'll keep the knife in my boot, though. Just in case something else comes at me out of the dark."

She trots off to the south, following her nose to find his trail and following it about two miles away to the southwest. The scent is difficult to track at first because she has to rely on the faint whiffs the Alpha throws off just staying in one spot for a while. When she finally catches the scent of the Alpha on the branches of trees and on the ground, she knows she has finally found where he had walked to find his camping spot. Judging by the light breeze coming from the river behind her, she knows she is further south and upwind from her quarry, which is what she planned. She wants this Alpha to know she is coming. She wants him to be expecting her and wants him to know she doesn't mean to sneak up on him. She wants to talk to him and not to fight him.

*   *   *

Here we go. The Alpha, sitting in his own campsite about a mile and a half from where he senses the five humans are settling, hears and smells the approach of the Beta behind him. *Wonder what she wants.* He stands, his tall frame lean and powerfully built and perfect for wandering the area. He stretches his long legs and arms, loosening his joints and preparing his body for anything.

When the Beta is within quiet hailing distance but not quite close enough to see, he barks out a command. "Stay where you are!" The command rings with well-practiced authority and the Beta pauses.

"I'm not here as a threat." Her voice is strong, without a hint of fear or wariness. "I'm here as an emissary between you and my Alpha. We just want to talk to you."

"I've heard claims like those before," the Alpha responds, a hint of a growl in his voice. "Why should I trust you?"

"If you let me come a little closer, I could show you I am as unarmed as I can be considering where I am." She takes one step forward. "I have one knife in my boot for self-defense, but other than that, I left all my weaponry with my Alpha as a sign of trust. I am only here to talk."

"You may approach," he says at last, backing into a shadowed corner of the campsite and allowing the Beta to come into view. "I just hope you understand, I will be keeping my full identity hidden. I don't fully trust you yet."

"I understand your caution." She steps into the moonlight, facing him with her arms slightly raised, and her empty hands with the palms open. "My name is Zoya. I come from the Chicago Territory. My Alpha and I were sent on a mission to find more humans because our stock of humans is slowly running out. We are tailing and tracking this small band of humans to see if they will lead us to a larger supply of them."

A gruff snort escapes the Alpha's nose as he bites back a laugh. Zoya glances up and he answers her questioning gaze. "The Wise Alphas of the Chicago Territory still believe eating humans is the only way they can survive?" He scoffs and waves a hand dismissively. "If they took the time to live outside their precious cities for longer than one day, they'd learn about how animal flesh, while maybe not nearly as appetizing to smell, will fill your belly and keep you in the territories just as well."

He turns away from her to pace in the darkness a little before turning back. "My name is Abrahm. I am here to watch out for my daughter."

"Your daughter?" Zoya's voice is curious. "You mean the one who doesn't smell quite human? We were wondering what she was. You mean, she's an Alpha like you? She doesn't smell like one."

"She's why I'm here." Abrahm's sigh stops Zoya's questions. "She's latent. I don't know if she'll be an Alpha, but she will be a Lycan if she's ever bitten by one. She'll be triggered if exposed to Lycan DNA. But she doesn't know, so I'm here to make sure she stays safe if at all possible. If she does get bitten, I can take her away and teach her how to be a Lycan."

"She doesn't know?" Zoya's voice is incredulous. "Why doesn't she know? Was her mother human? Why didn't you change her before? She seems to hate Lycans. She was ruthless earlier today when she had to fight an Omega. What were you thinking, leaving her to be raised by humans?"

"I was thinking about how the life of a Roaming Alpha was not safe for a child." Abrahm's tone is dark, forbidding. "I was thinking, letting her be raised in a somewhat safe environment where she could learn to hunt and be independent would be good for her. I was there when her settlement got attacked by a huge pack of Omegas. I kept most of them away from her, but I couldn't keep them all away. She and her mother accidentally ran into a small band which had evaded me. Cleo was able to get away, but not before her mother was killed. That's why she hates Lycans. She'll need to learn what she is if she's ever bitten."

Abram looks up at Zoya with a glare. "I saw her fight the Omega you let slip past. She shouldn't have had to fight it at all if you and your Alpha hadn't gotten in my way. I was trying to stay away from you two and in doing so, I put my daughter in danger and almost had to take her from her friends. She could have been bitten."

"Hey, I fought them as best I could," Zoya defended herself. "I was sure the one who got past me was the lowest of the three. I killed the other two. He was so scared; I was positive he would blunder into her path without realizing what was happening and she could easily have killed him. There wasn't much of a risk."

"There is always a risk to anything you do." Abrahm's words are sharp. "Now, if you two are going to be of assistance to me, I need you to keep out of my way. Do not interfere with my daughter and her friends getting to the Northern Settlement."

"We originally planned to help them get there," Zoya interrupts Abrahm. "But what should we do about our mission? We were instructed to bring information about the human settlement to the Chicago Territory so an attack might be mounted, and the humans could be rounded up."

"Ask yourself. How have you two been surviving if you haven't been picking off these humans one by one? The meat you've been eating sustains you just as well as human meat does. If you can survive without eating human meat for days or weeks on end, the territories can survive on food other than human flesh."

Zoya frowns but nods slowly. "I will go back to Themis and let him know what you've told me." She gives a short incline of her head. "Thank you for your insight. You are more than welcome to join us if you wish. We are just on the eastern side of the humans' camp if you would like company."

Abrahm smiled at her offer and nodded. "I will think about it. I might move further north, now I know you are not—" His voice cuts off as a sound catches his attention and he looks toward the human's campsite.

"What—?"

"Shush!" Abrahm cuts off Zoya's question. He begins to transform, his ears growing more pointed and mobile, turning to the north to better catch the sounds his more human ears couldn't fully detect. Then he freezes. "Omegas," he mutters, stepping forward. "A huge pack of them. We need to move now!" And without another word, he darts from his hiding place and toward the abandoned church, Zoya hard on his heels, transforming on her way.

*   *   *

Stretched out on the grass and resting near where Cleo paces, Themis almost misses the faint sounds of approaching Lycans a few miles away. When he sits up and glances to the north, his ears perk forward to better catch the sounds. He shoots bolt upright and struggles to his feet, swearing softly. He dashes from his hiding place, away from the camp and toward the sound of the approaching Omegas.

Where is Zoya? He transforms himself into his wolf form. He gallops forward, hurrying to be the front-line fighter against the incoming horde of Lycans coming for the small band of humans. Before he runs ten minutes, he comes across the front scouts of the pack of Omegas. He slows down and plants himself directly in their path, a snarl curling his lips from his bared fangs.

"*Leave!*" His roar is enough to give the three scouts pause. The thrum of power in his voice indicates his strength and prowess at fighting. "*Leave now and you won't have to die.*"

The three look at each other, their lean bodies and hungry eyes give Themis an indication of just how desperate they have become. In some of the faces, patches of weeping sores reveal how some of them have even started to pick off and eat their fellow Omegas.

"Let's kill this Alpha whore!" the scout in front barks to his fellows. *"I don't feel like sharing a meal with the likes of him."*

"I warned you," Themis rumbles, crouching in a prepared stance. Before he can say more, the Omega in the center and the one to the right leap forward with their claws extended, fangs dripping with expectant saliva. Themis charges forward, raking the first Omega to reach him in the snout with his left paw, the second with his right. Both are turned away dripping blood from deep gashes in their faces. The third Omega paces to the right a little bit, as if to try and get behind Themis, but Themis anticipates his moves and lunges, getting his jaws around the weaker creature's foreleg to crunch the bone. Themis feels the satisfying snap in his mouth along with the rank taste of Omega blood. He shakes the creature off before throwing it to the ground.

He turns and immediately guns for one of the other Omegas' throats, ripping it out before the third can jump on top of him. Themis then spins around to rip his claws into the exposed belly of the final scout.

Themis ducks and retreats a few paces back toward the human encampment to survey the carnage of the one wounded, the one dying, and the one dead Omega at his feet. The wounded pack member whines piteously as Themis stalks forward for the kill, but hardly makes a sound when Themis's jaws clamp around his neck and shakes it violently, feeling the bones in the neck snap.

Themis turns again at the sound of rustling tree branches and nearly springs at the approaching figure before recognizing Zoya, fully transformed and growling a challenge.

"Scouts." He doesn't bother changing back to his more human form to talk. He can hear the pack approaching, less than a mile away. They would have to fight again soon. *"I took care of them. I think this may be one of the biggest packs we've seen before."* He tries to keep the concern and worry out of his voice.

"I think you may be right." An unfamiliar male voice comes from behind Zoya and Themis realizes the Alpha who had stayed so far away from their following spaces is now less than six feet away, still skulking in the shadows. *"Have you tried forcing them to turn away?"*

Themis looks at the shadowy, wolfish form in confusion. *"What do you mean, force them? I told them to leave, but they just attacked me. It's not like I could push them back the way they came."*

"You've never learned your true powers, have you?" The other Alpha glares at him. *"You can mentally control any Lycan below Alpha in status. Any Betas, Deltas, or Omegas are yours to control once you master the skill."* His words surprise Themis who regards him with deep skepticism.

"I think I would have noticed if I were able to tell other Lycans what to do," Themis replies. *"Zoya, go jump off a cliff,"* He directs this last statement at Zoya who looks at him with a skeptical, unfazed expression and rolls her eyes.

The other Alpha turns to Zoya and, without saying anything, stares at the Beta. Zoya stares back for a second, then turns and circles the bodies in the clearing twice before stopping and shaking her head like a dog shaking water out of its ears.

"*Jeez! I felt weird!*" she exclaims, pawing at her face and ears as if a lingering presence still echoes there. "*Don't ever do it to me again!*" she complains.

"*I'll have to teach you some other time.*" The Alpha glances toward the sounds growing slowly louder. The tramping of several dozen feet on bracken and the scrabbling of claws on rocks and tree branches begins to echo around them. "*For now, let us just plan on fighting our best fight and keeping these monsters away from my daughter and her friends.*"

Themis doesn't have a chance to reply or even allow his mind to wrap around the sense of his words. Almost without warning, a blurred, fast-moving shape darts from the trees and crashes head long into the waiting trio of Lycans.

Zoya meets it with a howl of rage and pent up energy. She had been fighting restlessness all through the trip, wanting to lope along and travel faster than these slow-moving humans. Now she was finally able to expend all the energy she had been holding pent up inside her.

Themis takes on the two following just behind the first, able to slice a throat open without even trying, before moving in on the second and catching it a glancing blow to the temple and stunning it. Taking advantage of its momentary inattention, he latches his teeth on the back of its neck and shakes it like a rag doll. The body goes limp and he drops it to move forward toward the swarming pack.

He watches the other Alpha who focuses on the Omegas moving to the left around the growing pile of carnage and runs to cut off the approaching group on the right. Zoya is already working her way through the knot of warily approaching Omegas in the center.

The fight grows slowly more intense as the Omegas realize there are only three, two Alphas and a Beta, protecting the humans. And so more pack members throw themselves at them. Themis realizes one in five run at him and manage to slip past him to move further toward the band of humans they are trying to protect. He hopes they have heard the racket from the first small wave of Omegas and are ready to fight their way out of the area.

At one point, Themis is pinned against a small brace of trees and the remains of a wall, with five Omegas jumping at his throat at once. He swipes wildly at the one on his left which seems the weakest and barrels through him, running a little bit more south and into more open ground to continue the fight. He turns and is able to catch the first Omega with a heavy swipe of his forearm, causing the weakened muscles and bones to snap from the force of his swing. He lashes out a clawed foot at the next incoming Omega and feels it connect with the creature's right shoulder. The bone snaps beneath the force of his kick and the Lycan drops to the ground, howling.

Zoya lets out a horrific snarl and Themis glances up briefly to see her rip into three Omegas at once, still managing to keep the beasts around her and not running past her to the humans. In his second or so of distraction, an Omega manages to latch onto Themis's upper right foreleg with its jaws. But the hold is poor and the enemy is barely able to sink his teeth into the tough skin through the fur on his arm before Themis feels the pressure. He takes a swing at the snout on his arm with his left hand, managing to rake his claws and catch the edge of its eyes. The Omega releases him and wheels away with a scream of pain.

Its fellows bear down on him, five or six of them coming at him in retaliation, but Themis is ready for them. He crouches, making himself small and giving the six figures less of a target to get a hold of before he lashes out with teeth, claws, and strong kicks from his hind legs. The snarling and snapping at his face and ears become nothing more than the buzz of persistent bees as he paws and bats the jaws and claws away from his own face to deal wound after wound to the continuingly crowding creatures.

Then suddenly, Themis finds himself free and no longer battling the Omegas. The Alpha who had been following the humans stands over him, his graying hair and fur is matted with blood and gore but boasts less than a half dozen small scrapes and cuts over his body.

"You okay?" he asks, his frame more human than wolf and his mouth able to wrap around human syllables once more. He reaches a hand down for Themis to grasp.

Themis sighs with relief as he himself transforms back to his human state and takes the offered hand. "Thanks," he says, catching his breath from the fight. "Where did they all go?"

"I didn't get all of them, but most of them headed northwest. There was a significant group who managed to get south before I could get a hold of them. We need to go. I'm concerned for the humans."

Zoya stands just over the Alpha's shoulder, still in her wolf state, ready to depart despite several large gashes on her arms and torso. *"I'm heading there now. Don't take too long."* And with that, she disappears south toward the humans' campsite.

CHAPTER FOUR

Cleo glances up from where she kneels, checking a snare near the entrance of the campsite, faint sounds of howling reaching her through the trees. She is on her feet in an instant and darts through the tree gap without hesitation.

"Everyone up!" she yells, knowing they are all sleeping lightly if they're sleeping at all. "We need to move. There's a pack of Lycans heading our way. I don't know why they're not here already, but I hear fighting and howls further north. They could be here any minute." She grabs her packed bag from where she had laid it before she had gone out to keep watch and throws it over one shoulder before struggling to get the second strap over her other arm.

Charlie is the first one up on his feet and ready to go with Elijah and Kiya fast behind him. It takes Charlie shaking Mandi awake and several prompts to get her moving and on her feet, and still even then it's almost as if she doesn't understand the urgency of their flight.

Cleo pokes her head out of the now abandoned campsite and spots the telltale shifting shadows of Lycans surrounding the area. She motions for her friends to follow her quickly. Mandi's pack is barely out of the campsite before the first of the beasts blunders from the trees.

Cleo, her bow already nocked and pulled, fires it directly into the approaching beast's heart—it only advances five paces from the edge of the thick trees before it falls forward, dead. Before more of the Lycans push their way out of the trees, Cleo rushes forward, pulling another arrow. Elijah and Charlie follow almost immediately with Kiya and Mandi pulling up the rear. All five have bows or crossbows out and loaded, ready for anything to jump out at them.

Again, Cleo is the first one to get a shot off as they make their charge north into the woods. An Omega leaps forward, eager to get a taste of human flesh after the fight he just managed to escape with only a small slash to his left haunch. Cleo feathers him once, then slips her bow over her shoulder and pulls her machete and a small dagger from her belt, charging an arrow into the reeling beast's right lung. She slashes swiftly and cleanly at his throat and leaves him to her companions to deal with if he wasn't one hundred percent dead when they got to him.

In her dash forward, Cleo knows it'll take more than one or two slashes to dispatch these Lycans. She leads with her left, not letting any of the approaching Lycans within two arms' length, but now there's a significant gap between her and her friends, thanks to the beasts forcing her hand. She spots Charlie at one point, pushing his way through a small band of six wolves, so focused on what he is doing he doesn't glance up at her when she tries to shout his name. Elijah's shout comes from further behind her and to the right, but Cleo can't tell if it was a shout of pain or triumph against a foe.

In a lull of the press of Lycans, Cleo gets the chance to glance around her to spot Mandi and Kiya battling it out together, but Kiya seems to be unable to keep the beasts away from her. Mandi, on the other hand, is coming out ahead of her attackers. Cleo spots one of the lurking beasts at her left side, preparing to leap, but before she can shout out a warning to her friend, another wave of Lycans diverts her attention and pushes her further west and away.

Due to an instant of inattention, Cleo shrieks in pain as a claw digs into her right shoulder and down her back as she spins to dislodge it. She feels another flash of pain on her right side and an Omega stumbles away, its muzzle and forepaws covered in blood. She slashes at it and manages to get her machete stabbed into its side before it bolts, leaving her staggering.

Taking advantage of the sudden disappearance of Lycans in the area, Cleo glances up at the stars above her and trots as quickly as she can toward her friends continuing to struggle with Lycans—they're not fighting to win; they're fighting only to retreat and live another day.

Cleo darts forward and slices her way into the midst of the group of Lycans, wounding most of them. Doing a quick head count, Cleo notices they are short Kiya, but the sounds of growling behind them makes her certain they cannot stay here or go back to search for their friend.

"Let's get going!" she yells as the last of the Lycans who aren't wounded half-heartedly fight back. Her friends nod their agreement and turn to the north. Cleo becomes the rearguard as Charlie takes point and leads them north at a hurried trot. The footing is unsteady in the dark, but Cleo knows the further they move away from their once secure campsite and this mess of carnage, the more easily they'll be able to rest and recuperate before moving on in the morning or early afternoon the next day.

Charlie leads the group forward, keeping his eyes peeled and ears alert for the sounds of approaching Lycans. From what Cleo glimpses as she guards the back of the group, his body is tense and hard, his expression one of concern, anxiety, and a reluctance to be moving forward when one of their number is still not accounted for.

Cleo taps Elijah's shoulder and motions for him to take her position and they swap positions so Cleo can reach an arm out to Charlie.

"We need to keep moving or we'll be killed," she murmurs to him as her hand brushes his shoulder. "She's a strong fighter. She'll catch up with us as soon as she can. I'm sure she's just been delayed. She'll find us."

Charlie nods numbly, as his tense posture relaxes slightly. Now he is more focused on what he's doing. Cleo glances back to Elijah and nods to indicate she'll take her place at the back once again. Charlie leads them forward, finding his way to the edge of a huge, overgrown highway littered with abandoned, stripped, and plant-infested vehicles. The highway leads in a northward direction and Charlie finds a way to scramble down the crumbling wall blocking the road off from the surrounding landscape before turning to help the rest of the party down.

When Cleo descends the wall, Charlie says, "Your shoulder!" He glances at her blood-soaked and ripped T-shirt hanging off of her right side. "Cleo, why didn't you say anything?" He grabs at the pack, still miraculously attached to her, and pulls it from her back.

"It's fine for now," Cleo replies, but Charlie refuses to listen. He manages to wrench the pack from her, and Cleo lets out a sharp cry as feeling begins to creep back into the shoulder which hadn't pained her since the wound occurred. The adrenaline in her body has started to disappear and now she senses only the pain. All the other cuts and scrapes she hadn't noticed when she had been fighting now all burned hard, but they all paled in comparison to the huge gash in her right shoulder.

"We should be safe enough here for a few hours." Charlie glances around, not seeing any sign of Lycans. "Let's get settled and I can get this at least covered." Cleo smiles despite the pain and allows her little brother to guide her to a nearby boulder of cracked cement to sit down as he pulls off his own pack and begins digging into it, searching for medical supplies and anything he can use to cover the huge gash running from the top of Cleo's shoulder at about the halfway point between her neck and down to nearly her right hip.

Charlie gathers a strip of cloth from his bag and one of the waterskins and sets to work. He wets the strip and begins to dab lightly at the edges of the gash, unwilling to touch the raw open skin if possible.

"At least the bleeding has stopped for the most part," he mutters, dabbing at the slight trickle still oozing from the bottom of the scrape. "But I don't know how to cover this large of a wound. We don't have nearly enough fabric to cover it, and if you put a shirt over top of it, the shirt could be covered in blood in minutes if you move wrong and break open the newly formed scabs."

"Do what you can," Cleo responds, watching Elijah set up a fire pit for camp. "I will probably keep this shirt on for the time being, just because it is already ripped where it needs to be. Is it clean enough for me to be able to go to sleep for a while? I want all of us to sleep at least a few hours."

"I've done as much as I can," Charlie replies. "The gash is deep, though. I wouldn't be surprised if you have difficulty with different tasks for a while. I'm sure there was muscle damage but I don't know how bad it is. You should try to take it easy as much as possible for now."

"I'll be careful," Cleo replies as she turns, grabs her sleeping roll, and lays it out near where Elijah is building the fire.

*   *   *

"I think they're all finally gone." Themis glances toward where Zoya stands, still sniffing and listening intently for any sign of the creatures that had attacked the humans with such ferocity. "What do you think—um…" Themis glances at the other Alpha, turned north after the scent of the humans.

"My name is Abrahm," Abrahm offers. "And I think you're right. I believe they have finally given up the hunt of this band of humans."

"I think one of them is missing." Zoya looks north, following the scents from where the humans had fought their way to retreat. "I only smell three of them and your daughter."

Themis nods in understanding and then follows Abrahm toward the faint and growing fainter smell of human among the stench of dead and dying Lycans. They proceed only a few yards further before Abram stops with a groan and sighs. His posture slumps from the usually upright posture Themis has come to recognize as his typical stance. When he gets to Abrahm's shoulder, he understands why.

The body at their feet still retains the general shape and size it once had in life, but the features of the limbs, torso, and abdomen are rent with gaping holes. Strips of flesh have been torn away. The face, despite the severe mauling on the rest of the body, still retains its lifelike appearance, the eyes wide and staring with only a slight cut on the bottom lip of the open mouth to mar the young woman's beauty. The sack the humans use to sleep in is still attached to the top of her pack, beneath her body. Themis kneels beside the fallen girl and pulls the sack from the rest of the pack and places the ravaged body into it.

"What are you doing?" Zoya demands, a look of horror on her face as she thinks he means to eat the flesh of one of the humans they had been protecting.

"I'm going to take her and leave her for her companions to find," Themis replies without glancing up, continuing his work. Abrahm kneels across the body from him, seeing his plan to use the sleeping sack to hide the worst of the Omegas' damage. Together, the two men gently move the body into the sack and tie it up so the body won't fall out of the bag. Zoya grabs the pack.

"They'll want to know what happened to her, and they'll want the supplies she carried." He glances at the deer hide pack stained with blood and other unspeakable gore. She nods, sure it has protected the supplies inside from everything.

Together, the trio of Lycans begin their trek with the dead human, moving north along the trail the humans have taken until their scent is strong enough to warn them the humans are near enough to possibly hear or see them. At this point, they turn west, going wide around where they spot the humans making camp in the center of the wide, abandoned highway. Themis finds a way down to the road, just under a mile away from the camp and around a bend, out of sight. Themis is certain the humans will walk on this road because of the crumbling walls and better lines of sight into the distance. They won't need to keep as many guards, and they will be able to know pretty far in advance if anything is approaching them.

"Will they find her here? What if they decide to leave this road and go outside of the walls?" Zoya scans the surrounding terrain, as if searching for a sign of the humans' intentions.

"I don't think they'll leave the road, Zoya." Abrahm takes the pack from her, laying it at the dead woman's feet. "It will give them safety and security, at least here in the outskirts of the city. They'll follow it at least to the country roads. And if by some mischance they decide to leave the main road, we'll move the body again."

Zoya nods and turns to leave, but Themis hesitates, still kneeling beside the body. He has closed her eyes and mouth gently when he lay her down and now he smooths the hair back from her forehead. He sighs once before standing. All three of them leave the way they have come; Themis is the last one out of the depression where the road runs. He glances back at the still bundle in the middle of the road, suddenly realizing how, even with the smell of her blood in his nose, his hunger never once raised its head and tempted him to taste her flesh. He is still full after the dog meat he'd eaten the day before.

*   *   *

You're dreaming! Cleo asserts to herself as she darts through bushes and low-hanging branches, the howl of pursuing Lycans close behind her. *You're dreaming and you need to wake up!*

A flash of gray in front of her gives her the barest warning before a snarling Lycan comes barreling into her. She lashes out instinctively with the machete in her left hand, cutting its head off without hesitation. Ahead, she hears an eerily familiar cry spurring her forward faster than the howls had.

Through the trees, the shapes of log houses and hastily built shelters surrounded by broken fences loom like the ghosts of barely remembered dreams.

No! Cleo charges through the fence, following the cries to her childhood home. *No! Mom!* The word bursts from her lips at the door hanging off its hinges. "Mom!"

"Cleo!" another voice calls from behind her, but she doesn't deviate from her path. As she crosses the threshold, the rustle of furtive movement and cries turning to moans draws her on.

"No!" she screams as the image of her mother's mangled body flickers beneath three bestial shapes. She slices at one with her blade before her surroundings flash and she is running through the forest again, cutting down foes.

To her right, Kiya's face flashes once, twice, then disappears with a shriek of "Help!" but Cleo can't stop or she'll be overrun.

Wake up! she screams at herself, without making a sound. Again, and again she forces her way through wave after wave of Lycans; again and again her friends' faces flash to her left or right before disappearing, all screaming her name in panic.

"Cleo!" Charlie's voice startles her to wakefulness with a jolt going all the way to her toes. She sits bolt upright, nearly cracking foreheads with her brother. He throws himself backwards at her sudden movement. "Woah! Easy, it's just me." He puts a hand on her left shoulder for reassurance. "You were thrashing around. I thought maybe you were having a nightmare."

Breathing heavily, Cleo shudders in relief, touching her brother's shoulder with her hand in silent thanks.

"Mom?" he asks, reading the pain and fear in her face as well as she read his own. At her nod, he sighs. "Me too. Especially with everything that just happened. Are you all right?"

"I think so." Cleo sighs with the release of tension and sharing her fears. "I saw her just like the last time it happened.

I just couldn't save her." A tear beads at the corner of her right eye. Charlie brushes it away as it slips from between her lashes.

"I don't blame you for anything," Charlie says before she can say more. "Go back to sleep. Try to get a few more hours of rest before we get going again. I'll be right here for you." He pushes her gently back to lying in her bed roll before sitting back down.

Cleo nods and curls herself more comfortably before closing her eyes and drifting once more into sleep.

*   *   *

Elijah remembers his fight with the Lycans—he battled three of them at once, slashing with his machete and dagger, his crossbow strapped to his chest and hanging at his right side, not able to be put to good use. He frowned in concentration, able to stab one of the beasts in the middle of its back as it turned to snap at one of its fellows. He slashed at another with the machete, feeling the drag of the blade in his hand as he caught it across the creature's chest. He knocked the third away and sliced through its neck as he turned the blade aside in a vicious down cut. In his moment's breathing space, he saw Mandi and Kiya, battling close to each other. Mandi seemed capable of holding her own and beating the beasts surrounding her, but Kiya struggled to keep the monsters away. As if sensing weakness, Lycans between the two girls turned for Kiya while Mandi killed the last of the beasts near her with ease. Catching her breath, Mandi turned to watch Kiya's fight with keen indifference. Elijah watched as an Omega prepared itself on Kiya's left side and launched at her. Before he could shout out to warn her, a lone Omega forced Elijah to focus on the fight again and by the time he put the stubborn beast down, Kiya was killed, and Mandi was running north toward Charlie, while Cleo was fighting forward toward the others. Elijah bull rushed his way into the group of his fellow humans and continued to fight, unable to process exactly what he had seen.

When Cleo made her way to them, she shouted, "Let's go!" and they managed to fight their way through a potential massacre.

*   *   *

What did I see? Elijah now finishes packing up his gear. Cleo has woken just after sunrise with a scream of pain as she rolls onto her back and then wakes everyone else up. With everyone awake and still twitchy about the possibility of Lycans being close, they had all decided to pack up.

She and Kiya were fighting together. He knows he's right. He thinks back again to the scene. Kiya, struggling with five or six Lycans snapping and snarling. Mandi only had about three around her, and as soon as she had slashed and killed the closest to her, the other two had decided to go after easier prey. They had moved toward Kiya, yet Mandi hadn't done anything to go after them or kill them. She had just stood there, watching. Her face held a look of indifference he hated to see in others like she hadn't cared who won the fight. Then there had been an Omega to Kiya's left, her blind side. It had pounced on her. Mandi hadn't even opened her mouth. Elijah had tried to call out, but then he had been distracted. *Yes. That's what happened. So why didn't Mandi say something? Why didn't she charge the jumping wolf?*

The questions chase their way around his head as he finishes packing and takes his place in the group's lead. Cleo has said they will follow the roadway to keep their travel easier and keep the protection of the surrounding, crumbling wall within their sight. Bearing north, Elijah hears Cleo and Mandi behind him and Charlie in the back. Everyone is prepared as Cleo insists they move in a tighter formation because they don't have a fifth person anymore.

Their progress is steady, no longer a trot to get away from danger but a confident pace to keep everyone moving for longer during the day. The sun sits barely over the horizon, mostly blocked by the walls on their eastern side, so they don't have to squint as the light grows brighter. The first half a mile goes by when Elijah spots a long bundle lying in the middle of their path a little way away. His blood suddenly turns cold as he signals to his friends to pause. He jogs ahead to investigate. Before he is less than ten yards away, he knows what the bundle is and nearly stumbles in shock and despair. He signals for the others to follow and steps up to the body that shouldn't be lying here. *Who moved Kiya's body?*

He hears the gasps of his friends and the choked sob Charlie lets loose at the sight of his best friend and closest companion. Charlie pushes past him and kneels by Kiya's head, head bent, tear tracks visible in the dirt and blood smeared on his face. Elijah moves aside as Charlie's fumbling hand pushes him away. The silence is far too loud.

Cleo steps up behind her brother to look down at her former companion wrapped in her sleeping bag, her right hand pressed to her lips in grief and her left hand extended in solidarity with Charlie. Elijah notices Mandi is still behind him and turns to find her staring blankly at the body, her face completely expressionless and her body frozen. Elijah feels the hitch in the back of his own throat, yet he doesn't notice the same presence of grief in Mandi's chilly countenance in front of him. Her lack of expression almost seems to say, "What the hell is she doing here?"

Elijah's grief is burned away by fury at Mandi's lack of interest in the death of their friend. *No, it wasn't a figment of his battlefield scattered memory but the truth.* He deeply inhales to try and settle his nerves and turns back to Cleo and Charlie.

Cleo has knelt by Kiya, her wounded arm tucked tight against her side as her other hand gently grazes Kiya's forehead. Her lips move soundlessly in a prayer for the dead Elijah remembers from their time in the settlement. Cleo's eyes close and leak tears. When she finishes the prayer, she glances up at her remaining friends.

"We should bury her," Cleo states, her voice rough, congested with sorrow. "Eli, can you take Charlie to gather large stones?" At Elijah's nod, she turns to Mandi who, Elijah notices with scorn, has rallied her expression into one of sorrow which feels false and overly done. "Mandi, could you help me dig a small trench for the body? I'm not sure how much I'll be able to help with. I can't move my arm too well, and it hurts too much."

Mandi nods and immediately pulls her pack off and grabs a small trowel strapped to its side. "I'll take care of it. Just keep a look out." Everyone but Cleo jerks into motion at her words. Elijah takes Charlie's arm and helps him to his feet, and they go off toward one of the crumbling walls, looking for large chunks of rock and cement large enough to make a cairn.

Charlie moves in a dream-like state, barely looking where he is going, stumbling on small pebbles and brambles under his feet. One of these stumbles nearly drops him to the ground on his face and Elijah manages to catch him and settle him on a boulder.

"Charlie." Elijah's voice doesn't seem to be able to get much reaction out of the young man in front of him, so he gives his friend a shake to get his attention. Charlie stares up into Elijah's eyes with a look of such despair, Elijah's heart breaks anew at this small glance. "Charlie, man, I'm so sorry but I need you to come back to us." He gives Charlie a small shake. "I know you and Kiya were together. I know you're a mess right now and I'm sure you can't think past how she's gone, but Cleo and I need you. Mandi too. We're all struggling to get up to safety in the Northern Settlement and we need you to get there. We're all grieving, you especially, but we can't fall to pieces until we're behind a big, strong wall."

Charlie blinks several times and the tears slide. Elijah knows Charlie is struggling and wants to grieve for his love, but Elijah also knows they need to keep fighting with focus in order to get away from the remaining Lycans who might be hunting them as well as any other Lycans who may catch the scent of blood they left on the battleground.

"I need to know I can count on you being there for me when I fall asleep at night, leaving you to watch out for us when it is your turn at guard. I need to know you will be able to focus on the surroundings and alert us if you hear or see anything that looks like Lycans. I need to know you won't go off on a hunt alone and get yourself killed so you don't have to go another day without Kiya." Elijah shakes him with each new thing he needs to know from his friend. Each time, Charlie gives him a bit more sign of life. "I know you're hurting, but I need you to keep your hurt bottled away until we can all get to safety. Your sister would be devastated if you disappeared. She's torn up about Kiya just as much as you are. She knew how much you guys loved each other. You both just lost your mother and now Kiya. You have every right to be upset. But Cleo will be putting on a brave face for you. She needs you to do the same for her." With this last line of thought, Charlie comes back to himself, the thought of his sister having to struggle on with the grief of their mother's, Kiya's, and his own death.

"Let's go." Charlie's voice startles Elijah a little. "Let's get the rocks so we can move forward." And without another word, Charlie stands and grabs as many large stones as he can. Elijah collects an armload of his own and follows his friend back to where the girls wait. Mandi continues digging a two-by-three-foot trench with a depth of only six inches.

Charlie grabs his own trowel and kneels to help deepen the hole a bit while Elijah goes off in search of more stones. It takes about three more trips for stones before the trench is almost long and deep enough for Kiya to be laid inside it.

Elijah and Charlie move her body with exceeding care, laying her in the middle of the trench. Then comes the slow process of covering her body with stones. Charlie does most of this work by himself, leaving Cleo, Elijah, and Mandi to stand guard, go through Kiya's pack they had found at her feet and redistribute all of the materials from the pack among the three other packs.

Despite the great amount of blood soaked into her pack, none of the supplies inside had been touched by the bearer's blood and everything was worth keeping. Cleo handles most of the redistributing, but when it came time to put her own pack back on after Charlie had finished covering Kiya with stones, she could only support the weight of the bag on her left shoulder because of the gash on her right. She stubbornly refuses to let anyone carry her pack, but Elijah knows she won't be able to go for nearly as long as the rest of them with the pack only supported by one shoulder, especially now with the added weight.

"I know you feel you can keep the pack on and keep going the same as the rest of us," Elijah states blatantly, standing in front of her so she can't start walking north along the road again. "But you're hurt. Let us carry your bag. We'll take turns carrying it so one of us isn't slowed down by the double pack, but it will also allow your shoulder to continue to heal and keep your body from getting overtaxed. We need you to lead us. Without you, we'd be lost."

And finally, with much huffing and complaining about how she feels useless, Cleo hands her pack off to Charlie who hoists it onto his front like a bizarre pack animal and grimaces at his sister.

"You're allowed to feel useless for now," he chides her, taking up his position in the back of the group. "We'll expect you to be back at full force again in the next few days. Until then, just be extra vigilant and let us know if you see anything. Doesn't matter how insignificant it seems, let us know and we'll check it out." Charlie nods to Elijah and the group moves on, leaving their fallen comrade buried under a pile of stones, a small wooden cross marking her head and a small bouquet of wildflowers over her chest.

Elijah had peeked beneath the sleeping bag when Charlie was focused on his digging. He hoped no one else looked at Kiya in this state. The sight had been gruesome, and he was thoroughly relieved to have escaped from the carnage intact. Just the sight of the wound on Cleo's back is enough to remind him of how savage the creatures they battled were. He didn't want Charlie dwelling on the thought of how much pain Kiya had been in when she died. He wants him to remember her as he had last seen her, ready for a fight and full of life. The formation of humans treks slowly down to the level road, stopping every hour or so to take a break for water and a bit of food.

Elijah takes Cleo's pack after the first stop and passes it off to Mandi after the second. He notices at each pause how Cleo's eyes begin to shine brightly with the hints of fever. At the third stop when Charlie takes Cleo's pack, Elijah's forearm brushes accidently against her upper right arm and she jumps back with a cry, as if scalded. Elijah is startled to feel how warm her injured arm is. He manages to clutch at Cleo's uninjured left arm.

"What's wrong?" he asks, noticing even her uninjured arm is hot to the touch. He brushes his fingers against her forehead and cheeks to find the fever there as well. "You're burning up!" he exclaims, pushing Cleo toward the hood of a car to lean against it. "Why didn't you tell us you were feeling feverish? We could have stopped to help you."

He glances toward Charlie who stands to Cleo's right, examining the uncovered gash through the rent in her shirt. Charlie sounds worried and defeated when he says, "The gash is swelling, but I don't see any pus and it looks like the wound has scabbed over in the night. I think it might just be her body's way of dealing with the wound and trying to keep her healthy by burning away any infecting bugs, but I really don't know. There isn't anything I can do."

"I'm sure I'll be fine later," Cleo says, trying to push away Elijah's worried hands. "I just need a little bit of water and I'll be ready to continue on." She lifts a waterskin to her lips and takes a few small pulls of the water and replaces the cork. She also takes a strip of jerky from Elijah but doesn't bite into it, just holds it and stands as if trying to pushing herself on. Elijah sighs reluctantly and they start moving again.

At each of the next two stops, he makes sure Cleo drinks water and takes a few bites of the deer jerky in her hand. He notices she doesn't eat while they walk and every time she takes a bite while he watches, she seems to turn slightly green. She forces the meat down as if knowing she needs the nutrients but seems more and more reluctant to swallow the tough flesh.

At their fifth stop, Elijah calls a halt for the day and decides to make camp on the road again. There is an opening into a forest nearby where he hears a stream which means possible options for hunting. Cleo sees the trees and makes a beeline for them.

"I want to see if I can set up a few snares," she says, pulling a small pouch from her pack where Mandi sets it down. "I'll be back in a little while." And without another word, she disappears into the trees. Elijah, Charlie, and Mandi begin to set up camp and Elijah asks Charlie to start a fire while he and Mandi load the waterskins on their arms searching for the source of the rushing water.

Once the pair of them are out of sight behind a wall and several dozen trees, Elijah rounds on Mandi and pins her to a tree. His dark glare is enough to keep her from making any sounds of protest.

"Tell me what really happened back there at the fight," he demands. "I saw you and Kiya. I saw you fight your way free from them, and then watch without a word as Kiya was pounced on from her blind side. Tell me I'm wrong. Tell me I didn't see you let Charlie's best friend die. Tell me I didn't see you heartlessly allow one of your own kind be devoured by the creatures we are trying to fight. Tell me all of this was just a trick of my mind because I was fighting off Lycans of my own and must have miss-seen what happened." Even as he says these words, he sees her lack of empathy and interest in what he is saying, and he knows his suspicions are right.

Mandi just looks at him, her moss green eyes impassive. Her expression alone gives him all the answer he needs, but even so, he still lets her speak.

"What do you want me to say?" She rolls her eyes. "Yes, I let her die. I didn't really care one way or the other. I had just gotten free of the stupid beasts. They were all over me, and she was mostly responsible for it. When it seemed like I was more likely to give a better fight for my life than Kiya, they all went for her and I was able to get away without more than a few scratches. So what? She's dead. There's nothing we can do now. We buried her, though I have no idea how she got in front of us. Especially judging by her injuries. She wasn't alive at the spot where we found her. Someone laid her in the road so we would find her. Whoever it was, they are likely still tracking us. That's what we should be focusing on. Not on why I did whatever I did. Now get off my ass about it and let's get some water and go back to camp. I'm hungry."

The casual way she just brushes off having let Kiya die drives Elijah to shove her violently against the tree again. "If you ever think any of the rest of us are so expendable as you obviously found Kiya to be, just remember: if it's not me you let get killed, I will be there immediately afterwards to kill you." He puts his face right in front of hers. "Do I make myself clear?"

"Crystal," she snaps back, pushing him away from her, moving to follow the sound of the water. Elijah follows, keeping a close watch on the surrounding woods and wondering just what might happen tomorrow.

CHAPTER FIVE

She's been bitten. The knowledge is certain as soon as Abram catches a whiff of Cleo's scent as she walks away from camp toward the forest. He sees the huge gash down her back and wonders if the bite might somehow have gone unnoticed in the jagged slash made by tooth and claws during the battle. *The transformation's already begun. I need to get her now before she becomes aware of her more acute senses and drives her friends away from my, Themis's, and Zoya's unfamiliar scents.* He watches as his daughter trots deliberately over the wooded terrain. Despite the injury that mars her shoulder and the fever that Abram can see in her eyes, she moves with an uncommon grace not usually attributed to humans, at least not those he has met.

She moves further away from the protection of her friends and into the wilder parts of the woods, setting up snares for unwary prey and takes breaks to sigh deeply. On impulse, Abrahm moves closer and closer to her, managing to get within six yards of her before she pauses and glances around her, as if sensing she is not quite alone.

She looks around and turns away from him for an instant and that's when Abrahm takes his chance. He darts out, grabs her around the waist and then clamps his hand over her mouth. He then takes off with her further into the woods where Themis and Zoya sit, discussing in lowered voices the possibilities for their future.

When Abrahm is sure that they are far enough away from the human camp that Cleo's screams won't be heard, he slows his pace and stops. When he sets the struggling girl on her feet in front of him and steps back, he is unsurprised to find a dagger blade inches from his face. He takes a slight step back and raises his hands to show his lack of a weapon.

"I don't want to hurt you." Abrahm keeps his voice low, steady, and unthreatening. "My name is Abrahm. I want to try to help you if I can."

"I don't care who you are." Cleo's voice is high, strained and there is fear barely constrained in her words. "I don't much care what you want. I want to know how you found me and my friends, and I want you to stop following us. If you don't, I will kill you."

These words bring a slight smirk to his face. Of course his daughter is spirited enough to threaten anyone when she is in the middle of a threatening situation herself. She reminds him of her mother who was so full of spirit that she willingly took him into her bed despite having a lurking suspicion of what he was. He never told her, but she had this way of looking at him, and he could just tell that she knew what he was.

"Don't you laugh at me!" she shouts, moving forward just a step, but the menace in that movement is clear. Abrahm notices that Zoya and Themis glance up at the girl's voice, but they don't start moving toward where Abrahm stands.

"I was not laughing at you," Abrahm clarifies, bowing his head in acknowledgement of her superior armament. "I was simply smiling at how much you remind me of your mother." Cleo's eyes narrow and she moves forward again, laying her blade against his throat as there is a tree trunk keeping him from backing up any further. He watches her eyes flick up and down his strangely garbed body, taking in the kilted animal skins, and open-chested vest across his torso. "You don't know my mother. You're one of the monsters that killed her. She never knew any of your kind and there is no way you would have ever met my mother." The rage and pain in her eyes are clear.

"I knew your mother about a year before you were born," Abrahm replies calmly. "I joined her community, searching for a bit of safety from those that were hunting me. Your mother found me, wounded on the outskirts of the settlement where she was living. She cared for me and nursed me back to myself. She was exceptionally kind and willing to give herself freely to anyone who needed help."

Cleo hesitates at the correct details in this description and this spurs Abrahm to continue. "When I was healthy and healed enough, we had grown close. She was beautiful with a gorgeous mane of curly auburn hair that seems to have been passed down in part to you. Your hair may not be curly, but it is certainly the same color as your mother's. You also share her heart-shaped face. Unfortunately, you got my nose and eyes." A grin spreads unconsciously on Abrahm's face and Cleo seems to unknowingly mimic it. She lowers her dagger and takes a step back.

"If you knew my mother," she starts, her voice hesitant, "what did she think of Lycans?"

"She never told me her views on Lycans in general." Abrahm continues to smile at Cleo. "But she did say before I left that if someone out there was like me, they couldn't be all bad."

As if sensing his true intention not to hurt her at last, Cleo sheaths the blade and steps away from Abrahm, a look of deep confusion and fever on her face.

"Before you start asking questions, allow me to give you a little bit of information that may or may not answer most of your questions," Abrahm begins, motioning Cleo to sit on the remains of a crumbled wall behind her as he sits himself on a large boulder. "Now, to start off, I would appreciate it if you don't interrupt. It will make everything go a lot smoother. When I say I knew your mother, yes, I knew her intimately. I am your father and have been looking after you since you were born. Yes, I am a Lycan as you guessed. I am what is known as an Alpha. I am one of the highest-ranking subtypes of Lycan that infest this world. I have been following you since you left the Tennessee Settlement, and I buried your mother after you had left. She is resting beneath a pile of stones, just like your friend who was killed by Omegas yesterday.

"As for the reason I've been following you, you are what is called a latent Lycan. Because you are your mother's and my daughter, you are half human, half Lycan." Cleo opens her mouth, but he plows through her protests. "Before you start arguing that you are human, listen. You were born with solely human traits, yes, but you have a distinctive smell. I don't mean you stink; you just smell different to Lycans. You don't smell quite human, but you don't smell quite Lycan, either. You've been able to live your whole life as a human because of the fact that you are latent. I have been keeping an eye on you to make sure that you were never bitten by a Lycan. If you were to be bitten, I would have immediately kidnapped you and stolen you away because you would have begun to change as you are now changing."

At this Cleo bursts out, standing and arguing unable to contain herself. "I am not changing. I just got scratched. I have a fever from the gash on my back, that's all! I'm not a latent anything. I am human!" In her anger, she pounds her fists on the wall. Abrahm notices her wince and tuck her right arm against her body again.

"The gash on your back was caused by an Omega grabbing you with its jaws, and then raking your back with its forepaws," Abrahm says when Cleo quiets again. "I've seen this kind of wound before, and most of the time it is far more deadly than it was with you. Omegas use this technique to incapacitate a human's arms so they can't keep fighting. Once unable to use one side or the other, the pack can more easily take the human down and eat it. Now, because you were able to dislodge the beast that grabbed you, you were able to fight your way out of the pack's grip. You and your friends were lucky; even with the death of your brother's girlfriend."

"You knew about her?" Cleo interrupts again, looking up with the ghost of tears in her eyes. "Were you the one who placed her out on the road?"

"No, that was Themis," Abrahm replies. "He is another Alpha that I have only recently begun to travel and work with. He and his Beta, Zoya, have been following you and your friends since you crossed the bridge into the city. They have been helping keep you and your friends safe. They've been patrolling ahead of you to keep the Omegas in the area as far away from you all as possible. Now all three of us will be patrolling, keeping your friends safe. The most important thing right now is you."

"What about me?" Cleo asks, looking suddenly wary. "If you're going to say I'm a latent Lycan again, you can forget it. I'm not transforming. I'm just a little sick from the scratch on my back. I'll be fine in a few days."

"You've stopped being able to eat the deer jerky your friend made a few days ago, haven't you?" Abrahm asks her when she stops talking. "The taste of the cooked meat makes you feel sick. You can smell your friends a lot more than you could before the fight too. Each person now has a distinct smell, don't they? That should be enough to alert you right there, but I'll keep going. You can hear the blood rushing through their major veins and arteries, can't you?"

Cleo shudders but Abrahm continues. "It is an enticing sound, isn't it? There's part of you that wants to turn around and sink your teeth into one of your friends' necks and taste the raw meat and fresh blood. I'm impressed you haven't succumbed to that drive yet. It shows just how strong you really are."

"But I don't want to be this." Cleo's voice waivers, her shoulders slumping forward as if under the great weight of this change. "Lycans killed my mother. I would rather die than be a Lycan myself. They are monsters. I want nothing to do with them!"

"I'm a Lycan," Abrahm says, his voice low. "I'm sure you noticed that when I was running you over to where we are now. I'm your father, biologically speaking at least. I may not have been there for you like the father who raised you, but I was the man who gave you life." He sees her watching him, with a look of mild disgust on her face.

"And I can tell you with one hundred percent truth that I have not eaten a human in over thirty years. I was born in a territory, so I was raised on human meat and therefore can't claim that I've never tasted human flesh, but I felt disgusted by the teaching that we needed to eat human meat to survive. I didn't think it was fair that a creature with the same amount of life and consciousness and ability as we had could be treated like cattle. So, I left my territory and decided to go it alone. It took me several times to learn how to catch prey, but I learned. I was able to keep myself fed. I met other Alphas who felt the same way I did, and we traveled for a while together. I learned that I could live off just about any meat I chose to eat. I learned that the Alphas in charge of the territories simply want to be in control of the whole continent and be able to keep everyone under their thumb. That is part of why I am here. I want to teach you so that you can grow up without having to taste human flesh at all. I want you to have the life I never had as a Lycan growing up in a territory."

At this point, Cleo trembles uncontrollably, her figure almost vibrating as he looks at her. She seems to be absorbing his words, but her face still holds a look of distaste. "So, you're going to try to teach me?" she asks when her voice is steady enough.

"Yes." Abrahm nods. "The first lesson you need to learn is the most important if you are going to continue to travel with your friends." She seems to perk up a little bit at this statement.

"You mean I can still travel with them?" she asks, looking incredulous. "I don't have to disappear all of a sudden?"

"You'll need to cover your shoulder here today or tomorrow," Abrahm says, looking at the gash. "But if you do as I say, there shouldn't be a problem with you continuing to travel with your friends. Your shoulder is already healing relatively rapidly. A few more days and you'll hardly know you were injured. That's one of the positives of being a Lycan, especially if you're an Alpha. Your healing abilities are several times faster than a human's. Your wound will be gone in about five days. There will be a scar, but other than that, you'll have no lasting effects from it. You might even be able to put a shirt on it now. The pain should be pretty bearable."

Cleo glances to her shoulder and shrugs it experimentally, smiling when she finds that there is no pain. "Wow. That will be incredibly helpful."

"Now, you need to focus." Abrahm turns and begins to pace slowly in front of her. "While you are with your friends, you need to keep your thoughts human. You need to be reasoned, focused on your goal and able to work through problems. Thinking in English often helps because a Lycan's mouth can't usually form the words of English when they are transformed. Some Omegas are able to speak broken statements because they spent several years learning how, but more often than not, they communicate in the guttural growling and body language."

"So, all I need to do to go unnoticed by my friends is 'think human?'" The note of a laugh seems to creep into Cleo's voice as she watches Abrahm pace. "That shouldn't be too hard, seeing as I've been human all of my life."

"You'd be surprised how unexpectedly the instincts of Lycans will creep up on you," Abrahm warns. "Even now, when you're not fully triggered, you might be able to transform at least partially into your true form." He keeps to himself the thought that if she does transform, she might never be able to regain her true human form. He still isn't one hundred percent sure what kind of Lycan she is. There is a good chance she could be a Beta like Zoya or even a Delta. He hoped for her sake that she was at least a Beta. She might be able to get north without her friends noticing. *If they're really unobservant,* a snide little voice in his head whispers. *Otherwise, they'll kill her the first time she starts to show.*

He decides against testing her control, praying that he will have the chance to test her before she and her friends come up against a true test and she goes full wolf right in front of them. He shudders involuntarily at the thought.

"What?" Cleo asks, glancing around. "Did you hear something? I didn't, and trust me, I've been trying not to hear everything that has been going on for the last however long you've had me here."

"No, I just felt a bit of a shudder," Abrahm soothes her. "Now I had better get you back to where you can be in easy calling range of your friends. I might be able to get you a few rabbits for dinner if you'd like, before you go back. That can be your excuse for going off on your own for so long."

Cleo grins a little sheepishly. "That's what I told my friends I was doing anyways," she admits. "When I left camp. I just needed to get away from everyone. It was getting to be too much."

"How about we plan on meeting together every evening after you make camp," Abrahm suggests. "That way, you can continue to make the excuse of going hunting and we can always grab a few rabbits in the woods before you go back to rejoin your friends."

"That sounds good." Cleo nods, smiling slightly despite herself. "Well, I'd better get back. Could you point me in the right direction?"

"I'll take you part of the way myself." Abrahm motions to the southeast. "After you." He takes a quick pause to listen to their surroundings in case random Lycans in the area follow Cleo closely.

Abrahm leaves Cleo less than a half mile from where she had left the campsite but keeps an ear on her until she makes it through the wall blocking the main road off from the forest surrounding it. Once ensuring her safety, Abrahm turns to find his own meal for the night.

*   *   *

"He's got Cleo." Zoya sits up from where she had been sprawled after a long day's trek. "What is he doing with her?" She cocks her head to listen and Themis pushes himself up too.

"What do you mean?" Themis turns his own head to catch the sounds of Abrahm and the squawks of a protesting girl in his arms. He recognizes Cleo's voice immediately. "What does he think he's doing with her? She's going to blab about us to all her human friends and we'll never get close to them again! We need to stop him." Themis stands up and moves to follow the slowly fading protestations, but Zoya grabs his shoulder and forces him to sit back down again.

"I think he's just telling her that he's her father and that he's here to protect them from afar." Zoya cocks her head and keeps an ear out for any trouble. "Now, we should get a little rest while Abrahm is chatting. I don't fancy being up all night with limited sleep during the day, do you?" She smiles to cut the bite out of her words and softens her face to try and get Themis to relax.

"I'm still not sure about this," he complains, moving to stand despite Zoya's rolled eyes. "I just don't feel comfortable about them talking. And I've noticed something else too." He looks Zoya in the face. "Cleo's scent is different. Haven't you noticed?"

"Of course I noticed," Zoya says, rolling onto her back and sitting up to better talk with her Alpha. "She's not fully human. Abrahm told us that." But she too had noticed that during the last twenty-four hours, Cleo's scent has changed. It no longer smelled like human and Lycan equally mixed. Now she was starting to get a more noticeable scent and it wasn't more human.

"You know what I mean," Themis interrupts, turning to pace in their small clearing. "She's starting to smell more like a Lycan. I'm worried she might be changing, like Abrahm was trying to prevent."

"I did notice she has a huge gash on her shoulder," Zoya points out. "It looks like one of the Omegas decided to try and rip her down, but she was too strong for them. One of them must have bitten her at some point during the fight."

"But what does that mean for our goal of protecting them now?" Themis asks, gazing at where the human camp is visible just through the trees. "Do we need to protect the three normal humans from Cleo? Will she need even more protection while she changes?"

"I'm sure Abrahm will explain what is going on when he gets back." Zoya lies back down. "Now, I'm going to take a nap while we wait. You might want to do the same."

Themis nods and leans against a tree. "I'll take a nap over here. Just to keep an ear out." And with that, the two young Lycans drift off into soft dozes. Their sleep stays uninterrupted for over an hour as the light grows dimmer around their little campsite. As the sun sets beyond the western horizon, Zoya starts from her sleep, suddenly aware of how dark it had really gotten and the chill that now sits around them. A crack of twigs snapping underfoot has her on her feet in seconds, already halfway transformed before she notices the scent of Abrahm that helps her breathe normally.

"Good to see you two getting your rest," Abrahm rumbles in a laugh at Themis struggling still half asleep to his feet. "I brought a bit of deer for you both. I got lucky and the deer wasn't that fast." He holds up two large chunks of raw, still bloody meat.

Zoya, the closer to him, grabs her chunk first and transforms to her wolf-self to eat, ripping into the flesh without care. Themis takes his time to wake up before taking his own chunk of the flesh.

"Thank you," he says simply before also transforming himself to eat. Zoya sits licking her hands and claws before glancing to Abrahm again, finished with her meal but waiting for Themis to finish so they can clean each other as is their custom after eating.

"Where did you catch the deer?" she asks, preferring to use the wolfish speech instead of transforming back to her more human form and feeling the stickiness of the drying blood. *"Aren't deer usually too fast for us to run down? I know I've never caught a deer. The only other time I've had deer meat was when Cleo shot down the deer when they had just reached the city."*

"Usually, yes." Abrahm nods, a grin playing on his lips. "But when the deer in question has an arrow in its chest, it isn't all that difficult to catch. Cleo shot the deer; I just ran it down and helped her get the meat and skin. Her friend was talking about how he wanted to keep the skins to dry them out and use them."

"We had noticed you were with Cleo." Themis swallows his last chunk of meat and begins to clean himself as well.

"What were you doing with her? Just hunting? Did you tell her what you are? What about what she is?"

Abrahm's wince makes Zoya feel bad about the suppositions she and Themis had made before their nap, but Abrahm nods and begins to speak almost immediately.

"Cleo is transforming into a Lycan," he says. "I don't know what kind yet. It usually isn't until the last day of transformation that you can tell what variant of Lycan a latent will be. She is likely only about two days away from her first full transformation, and I am hoping that she will at the least be a Beta. She might be able to pass as human, but if she is a Delta or God forbid an Omega, she will likely have to run away from her friends. I need you two to help me ensure that their daily walks go as smoothly as possible. If Cleo begins to transform, I need one of you to either 'kidnap' her or distract the others long enough for Cleo to be extricated as fast as possible. It is imperative that Cleo's transformation remain as unknown as possible to her friends."

"And how is that going to work?" Themis asks, transforming back to his human form after he and Zoya had groomed each other's faces. "I think they might start to notice that she has fur all over her body and only eats raw meat."

"She and I have talked over the details." Abrahm nods at Themis. "She will be taking nightly lessons with me when they first make camp every evening. I will be able to teach her how to control the wolf side of her body and how to look and act completely human. You would be welcome to these lessons too. I would like you both to learn a little bit more about yourselves. You can act human and become almost completely human with a little effort and time."

"So, you are planning to teach Cleo these lessons in the hopes that she first transforms while she's with you?" Zoya asks, ignoring the offer to take Abrahm's "How to Be Human" class for the moment. "You hope that you will be able to control that transformation and teach her in one night how to go between human and wolf?" The sound of her skepticism is clear to everyone. "Do you know how long it took me to stop transforming whenever I was mad or hungry or even remotely upset? I don't think I had full control over myself until I was maybe sixteen or seventeen years old. It wasn't until then that I stopped spontaneously changing and then it took until I was close to twenty for anything stressful or challenging to stop fazing me. I'm only twenty-two. I still don't think I have full control over myself at times."

"The lessons I'm offering could help you with that control." Abrahm looks kindly at the Beta. "I had similar problems with control until I found someone to teach me. I never knew the kind of control I now have was even possible until I ran into a roaming Alpha who taught me just how much the right mental attitude and force of concentration can influence how you perceive situations and how you control your more bestial self."

"You think your teachings will make a brand new Lycan completely able to control herself after only one lesson?" Zoya repeats more succinctly, the sarcasm and scorn making everyone wince. "Yeah, right."

"I am not claiming that she will be completely in control," Abrahm says in response. "That is why I need you two to be extra vigilant about keeping anything out of their way. The less she must fight, the better. I need to keep her calm and as far from stressful situations as possible until she has gained the necessary control."

"You are going to be giving her nightly lessons." Themis cuts across whatever Zoya was thinking about saying. "And these lessons are open for us to join? Why would Cleo want to work with us? I thought she hated Lycans."

"She does." Abrahm sighs. "She will be fighting within herself for a long time to come to grips with the fact that she is now one of us. But I think by meeting us and seeing that we have some of the same instincts and protective behaviors that she has associated with only humans can change her mind. About some of us at least."

"You should get some sleep before we have to be on guard for the humans." Zoya nods toward a patch of springy grass and leaves. "We'll keep an ear out for now." And with that, she trots off around the human camp.

Who does he think he is? she asks herself, trying to keep her steps calm and even despite her raging thoughts. *I have been trying my damnedest to keep myself from blowing up at him ever since he got here, with his holier-than-thou-attitude. Why should we follow him? Just because he's a roaming Alpha and doesn't eat humans and thinks keeping his half human daughter like a pet and teaching her all about the Lycan ways is a good idea? He shouldn't be risking all of us just so that he can keep his daughter alive. We should bring all five of them to Chicago and let the Wise Alphas decide what to do with them.*

It takes Zoya a good two hours to pace herself into a stupor and by that time, night has truly fallen. The muted glow of the human fire gives her the chance to see three of the humans huddled there. Cleo is absent and must be in one of the tents set up nearby. Her brother pensively pokes at the fire with a long, thin stick. The glint of tears on his cheeks is the only sign that he mourns the loss of their fallen friend. The other two sit on either side of the brother, taking turns glaring at each other and eating the roasted steaks of deer meat that Cleo brought them from her hunt with Abrahm. The scene is almost surreal to Zoya who has never had the chance to learn what it means to be part of a family. Her pack was never more than four or five Betas and Deltas, eager only for the added power and ability to capture more humans, more prey. The pack never cared if you were having a bad day or didn't want to hunt humans. They just wanted you to keep bringing in kills and meat for them.

But do you really need a family? A nasty little voice sniggered in her ear. *I mean, if you stay with Themis, you have him. Maybe you could get back to Chicago and start a family with him. You don't need to tell the Wise Alphas that you found anything. Or you could say that the humans were killed by rogue Omegas and there was nothing you could do.*

"Zoya?" Themis's voice breaks her out of her conflict. "You okay?" He regards her with a questioning look as she walks into their small campsite.

"Yeah." She nods, stretching and yawning. "Just a bit tired." She sighs, curling up on the ground near the bottom of a tree. "I'm going to sleep for a few hours. You and Abrahm good to keep an eye out?"

"Not a problem." Abrahm steps up from where he had lay down two hours previously. "You should get some rest too, Themis. I'll wake you both when I need you to take the watch. I'll be fine." He rolls his head on his shoulders, getting a good stretch. "Sleep well."

And with that, he leaves Zoya and Themis to curl up and get some rest.

CHAPTER SIX

Can it only have been three days? Cleo wonders to herself as she leads her friends across a large area of broken-down houses and other sad ruins. These houses used to hold so much history. Who lived or died in them? What were the families like? What kind of dinner did they eat on a Tuesday? Her friends are planning to set up camp beside a lake less than a mile away, as she was watching them from afar, clearly hearing everything they said.

They had been walking steadily at about six hours per day since they reached the ruins of what she had learned was once called Cincinnati. Each evening of the two days after she had been kidnapped, she had been able to slip away under the pretext of hunting. The first night, she had been startled to find Abrahm joined by another man who said his name was Themis. He was there to learn just like she was. Apparently, Themis and the other Lycan she had heard with him the night before when Abrahm had kidnapped her were following Cleo and her friends. They never really said why they were following them, so Cleo assumed it was likely something negative, but she didn't care. She appreciated that there were Lycans keeping an ear and an eye out on the other Lycans that could easily kill and eat her and her friends.

"We think that part of why we haven't seen many Omegas around is because your scent is starting to become overwhelmingly Lycan and it overpowers that of the humans you are traveling with," Abrahm said during the first lesson. "It deters them from trying to attack humans because they don't want to entangle with Lycans."

"Wait, what are Omegas?" Cleo asked, frowning at the unfamiliar term. "I thought you all were Lycans. That's what we were taught anyways."

"Well, that's where I'll start the actual lesson, and Themis can let his imagination wander for a little bit." Abrahm grinned. "He's heard and learned all about this already. The first thing you need to know is that there are four different variants of Lycan."

Cleo cocked her head to the right, almost like a dog cocking its head at an owner shouting incomprehensible words. "Four variants? Is it like a hierarchy or something? I remember hearing that some animal species form hierarchies to distinguish leaders."

"Yes." Abrahm nodded. "The top variant are the Alphas. They are the strongest, most powerful and the most variable of the Lycans. Alphas can look completely human if they so choose. I employ this skill daily to be able to go in and out of human settlements without too many questions and without the alarmed panic that usually ensues when humans catch sight of lower Lycans."

"So, you are an Alpha?" Cleo looked at him critically. "When I first saw you, aside from the fact that you were able to pick me up like you did and were able to run with me, you looked like a normal human. Your shoulders are a little bit too wide to be properly proportioned, and your ears are just a little too high on your head. But most of those things are hardly noticeable." She turned to Themis. "You on the other hand, you look like a hairy version of a human. Your proportions are almost perfect for a human, except for your fur."

"That's why I'm here," Themis said, grinning at her comments. "Though I have to say, in the winter, the added protection of the fur is nice. Especially on cold, snowy nights."

"Yes, but that is off topic," Abrahm interjected, redirecting the conversation. "Now, the second variant of the Lycans are the Betas. Zoya is a Beta. Betas are just slightly under Alphas in their abilities. Most of the time, Betas can control their appearance to look human at a distance. But under scrutiny, they would be chased away from a human settlement. With proper guidance, though, Betas can control their appearance almost as well as an Alpha. I have seen two or three roaming with other Alphas who can make themselves almost perfectly human. It was quite amazing."

"So maybe if Zoya were to join the lessons, she might be able to pass as human?" Themis asked, turning toward Abrahm. "That would be great. Maybe then we could join the human settlement as well."

"Maybe." Abrahm turned away from Themis and continued. "After the Betas come the Deltas. Deltas are not as fortunate as Alphas or Betas. They constantly have the form of a Lycan. They can alter their faces to have the power of human speech but that is about it. Omegas are even worse, depending on how diluted the lineage is." Abrahm shuddered and went on. "You've only had experience with the lowest, most vile Omegas on this earth. The ones scavenging across the country are causing havoc. One of these days, all the Alphas in all the territories are going to need to hunt down all the packs that have formed up. They are just so out of control."

Themis snorted. "The Wise Alphas of the Chicago Territory have said before that the only time they would ever bestir themselves was if the Omegas started taking out members of the territory or began exploring within the territory boundaries. Other than that, the Chicago Alphas won't do shit."

"It might come to that," Abrahm countered, but before he could say more, Cleo interrupted their banter.

"What variant am I?" she asked, a slightly nervous tone to her voice. "I mean, I can't be a Delta if I am still human-shaped, right? I mean, I would be showing more obviously if I were a Delta, wouldn't I?" Her voice and eyes were pleading for her reasoning to be sound, but Abrahm's look of concern made her heart drop.

"There's a chance you could be any of the types," he said. "You could even be an Omega. An Alpha can sire any variant upon a human. Most of the time, he or she will have a Beta or a Delta child. On the rare occasions that he finds a strong human with the ability, the child is born an Alpha. But I really don't know. You won't start to 'show' your Lycan traits until you are triggered." Abrahm glanced hesitantly at Themis and then continued his thought. "I believe you are only a few days away from your complete transformation, and we want to try and control the transformation as much as possible."

"What do you mean, triggered?" Cleo's voice was apprehensive. "Transform? Gain control of myself? What does all of this mean?" She could feel her heart pounding.

"Take a few deep breaths, Cleo," Abrahm pleaded. "I need you in a calm head space for me to tell you everything. I need you to be able to take in the information without panicking. If you panic, you will bring on the transformation so much sooner than we want, and we won't be able to help you much until you can calm down."

Cleo clenched her eyes shut and took several deep and calming breaths. It took almost a full two minutes before her breathing and heart rate returned to normal and she opened her eyes. "Tell me everything." Her command was sharp, but she seemed in better control of herself.

And so Abrahm told her everything. About how she would need to be stressed to the point of transformation. About how Abrahm wasn't sure how long it would be until she transformed, but that it wouldn't take long based on the signs he had noticed. Her back had already completely healed from the bite and slash from the fight two days before. The fever she had started to get after the gash had stopped sending violent chills through her body, but her temperature stayed high. Abrahm explained that Lycans usually ran at several degrees warmer than humans because they needed the extra warmth to keep off the chill during winter nights.

Abrahm also explained that, until she transformed, he couldn't give her straight instructions on how to transform or "untransform" at will. It was all a bit jumbled into an attempt to keep her feeling and acting as human as possible. Abrahm gave directions to Themis as Cleo watched, astounded as he followed Abrahm's instructions and all the fur across his body slowly disappeared. His skin, pale from the lack of sun and from being covered by fur for so long, almost immediately toughened just from the exposure to fresh air.

By the time the first lesson was over, Cleo's head was spinning with all the new information. She went back to her friends with a few rabbits slung over her shoulder and a well of possibilities.

The second day had been the day of her first transformation. Cleo had followed Abrahm's trail to a clearing several miles away from where her friends were camping. Abrahm had told her the night before not to bring any weapons with her, but she had tucked a small knife into her belt as she had left, just as a precaution and to help her gut any small animals that got stuck in the snares.

As she entered the clearing, she heard a sharp snarling from the opposite side of the clearing and out burst a growling Omega. She recognized it by its loping, wolf-like gait and long, pointed snout. This one stumbled as it caught her scent and gazed warily at her. She could feel it sizing her up, judging if she were prey or another hunter. When she didn't move at it, it turned on her and began to charge. With the instincts of hundreds of hours of fighting experience with the hunting parties in the old settlement and the last few fights with the Omegas, Cleo yanked the knife from her belt and charged back at the monster, slashing at it with the blade. Its claws raked her arms and back as they circled and slashed at each other. Cursing, she slipped beneath the monster's outstretched arms and jammed the blade between its ribs. It shrieked and fell away, but not before Cleo had wrenched the blade from its body and resumed the attack. She barely heard the shouts behind her as Abrahm and Themis came tearing out of the trees. Cleo buried the blade home in the creature's heart before turning to see the two newcomers.

Abrahm had shouted about her not listening to him and bringing a blade when he had specifically told her not to. Themis was blabbering about how she could have been seriously hurt and that Abrahm shouldn't have tried something so dangerous so soon.

The only thing that penetrated Cleo's muddled brain at that point was that Abrahm had planned this whole stunt. She saw red for the first time in her life. She hadn't known what exactly was happening with her body, but she knew she felt so much power. She didn't care that Abrahm was her father. He had planned to set this horrible creature on his defenseless daughter and watch.

Themis saw her first and let out a wordless cry of amazement and horror. Cleo barely heard him because she only focused her gaze on Abrahm. Abrahm heard Themis's cry and looked at her. Their eyes met and for the first time, Cleo saw fear on the older Lycan's face.

Subconsciously, as if it didn't need her permission, just her rage, Cleo felt her body changing. Her arms lengthened, the shoulders broadening to accommodate the growth of muscle in her torso. Her torso curved slightly forward, and she moved in a shuffling crouch until her legs folded beneath her and she was able to lope with a deadly grace. Her face contorted, sharpening to a wolfish snout, better for snarling and growling at the object of her fury.

Abrahm transformed almost instantly as she leapt at him and he caught her deflecting blow to the side of the head as he jumped away. She shook her head like a dog dislodging water from its ears before turning to follow Abrahm.

"Cleo!" he barked at her and she was surprised to find that she could understand him. *"I only did this to try and help you. I wanted your first transformation to be in a controlled situation. I would never have allowed the Omega to kill you. I would have stepped in if it looked like you couldn't handle yourself."*

"Yeah, right," Cleo snapped back at him, barely able to make herself form the coherent words. She half saw Themis's shocked face as she spoke in the wolf tongue. *"Why don't you just leave me alone!"* She snarled again and lashed at Abrahm, catching him in the face once before turning tail and dashing into the trees, as far from the other Lycans as she could get while still able to keep an ear on her friends' campsite.

At that point, she remembered her friends and realized she couldn't return to them until she had learned how to transform back into her human form. She heard Abrahm and Themis talking together, wondering about what they should do.

"I can't hear her," Abrahm said. His voice was almost as clear as if he were standing beside her. "Which worries me. I didn't think she'd wander so far away from her friends."

"I don't think she's that far away," Themis cut in, and she heard him draw in a few sniffs. "Her scent is still pretty strong coming from upwind of us. I think she's got a stronger sense of hearing and of smell than we do. I'm almost sure she can hear everything we're doing right now."

"What makes you so sure?" Abrahm's voice was dubious. "I didn't get a good whiff of her when she left, and the wind just shifted again. Could you tell?"

"She's an Alpha all right." Themis's words made Cleo's constricted throat relax a bit. *Oh, she could hear them so well.* "One hundred percent, she's an Alpha. I got a really good whiff of her as she charged you and then when she bolted."

"Good." Abrahm sounded as relieved as Cleo felt. "Hopefully, she'll be able to calm down after a day or two and be able to return to us. She needs to learn how to turn back. I think she'll be stuck for a while."

Cleo took a deep breath and turned her focus to the camp of humans nearer at hand. Charlie was standing watch again. She needed to talk to him but dared not to venture closer to their camp than where she was now. Elijah and Mandi were discussing watches and who would take first and second. They knew, or thought they knew, that Cleo would want to take last watch or first watch when she got back, so if they decided on one of them to take first, Cleo would be able to get some much-needed sleep. Cleo sighed at the thought that her friends wouldn't be seeing her for a while.

Her focus on her friends and keeping up with them was so complete that she didn't hear Zoya until she came out of the trees. Cleo immediately jumped to a half crouch attack position before realizing that it was just Zoya.

"So, you've finally changed." She smirked, looking Cleo up and down. "Not bad. I'm impressed you managed to pull your father's Alpha genes up after all."

"Leave me alone," Cleo rumbled, her voice low and menacing. For an instant, Zoya looked like she would have loved to make a smart aleck comment, but in the next moment, Zoya was turning almost as if she had no control over her body and had slung off into the woods. Cleo felt a warm shudder run down her spine but shook it off.

She waited, an ear on her friends, as she settled into an uneasy doze. After almost an hour, she heard Abrahm's voice move closer to where Elijah and Charlie were still up chatting. She listened to the hurried rustle and clink of metal as the boys grabbed for weapons left lying as they heard the approaching stranger.

Elijah called out a challenge and Cleo heard Abrahm step out of the branches and into their line of sight.

"I'm not a threat," he called, and Cleo heard the distinct tensing of the bow string. "I've come with a message. I am a traveler; my companions found your friend suffering from a badly infected wound in her shoulder. We are treating her as best as we can. Your friend told me to find you and to tell you to move on northeast without her. She says she will catch up with you, and we plan to ensure she does. I will send word if problems arise and will bring her to you."

"How do we know you're telling us the truth?" Elijah snarled and Cleo had to smile. He was always the cautious one in their group. "What proof do you have that our friend was even with you or is still alive?"

"Cleo told me to tell you that she is doing a little better but is not yet ready to travel." She heard the small gasps of realization that he knew her name. "She said she'd race you to the destination if she had to, and that she'd win."

Charlie chuckled darkly. "I bet she would at that," he said before Cleo heard him address Abrahm. "Thank you for taking care of her. We look forward to having her back with us soon."

Cleo heard Abrahm turn and walk back through the brush and out of sight. She knew he was going to walk another half mile before transforming and joining back up with Themis and Zoya. She followed his progress until he met the other two Lycans and to settle down and fall asleep.

*   *   *

She watches her friends as they prepare their camp for the night, their words and movements more restricted and somber with the loss of first Kiya and now Cleo temporarily. Cleo hears Mandi complain about something and then Elijah barks at her to shut up and to keep working.

Further away, on the other side of the human camp, Cleo hears Zoya, Themis, and Abrahm settling into nap and rest after a long day of keeping ahead of the humans. They say Cleo has either lagged or sped up to get far ahead of the other Lycans.

You're going to need to go back to him, the little voice in her head reminds her for the umpteenth time that day. *He's the only one who can teach you to be human again.* The trouble is, she already felt more human. She keeps her thoughts on her friends now and she feels normal. Not that she hasn't felt normal throughout the trip. She is moving so much faster than she thought she was originally, and it is difficult to realize that she is outpacing her friends by several miles at a time. She doesn't feel like the monster who attacked Abrahm.

Cleo sighs and double checks where the Lycan camp is before setting off around the human camp. She hears the Lycans stir as she gets closer, but she walks straight into their camp on two feet without so much as a sound.

"Holy shit!" Themis exclaims as he stares at her, astonishment clear on his face. "Abrahm, have you ever seen this before?"

Even Abrahm's face, usually so composed, shifts from blank and white and then back again. "No." His voice is barely a whisper. "Never. I don't think even I have that much control." Zoya doesn't say anything.

Cleo frowns at the figures in front of her, confused. "What are you staring at? I've come to learn how to gain better control of myself. I want to get back to my friends."

"What do you mean?" Abrahm looks at her aghast. "You're human. You look completely human. I smelled you coming, but I never heard you. Yet you look completely human."

"What?" Cleo feels her face and looks down at what she had originally seen as claws. They still seemed claw-like to her own eyes and she frowned at them. "No, I don't. I still have claws for hands and I still feel like I have a great, long snout. I can't look human."

"Look at this," Zoya says, throwing a small, round flattened object at Cleo who catches it deftly despite it looking like her paws are doing the catching. She looks down in the mirror and sees her face staring back at her. The features seem a little rougher and leaner since the last time she had seen herself in a true mirror, but they still look like those of the human Cleo who had left the Nashville Settlement almost over three weeks before. A few long blinks later and her paws return to the shape of hands in her eyes.

Without looking at her stunned father and the other two Lycans, she drops the mirror and runs off toward the human campsite, the lightness in her chest filling her almost to the point of ecstasy.

*   *   *

"She's incredible." Themis hears Abrahm sigh as Cleo turns her back on them and flits away toward her friends and their campsite. "I've never seen anyone who could transform so completely as her. She doesn't look as though she's changed. She looks identical to how she looked when I saw her at the first lesson."

"I was certain it would take her weeks to complete the transformations and keep her appearance stable enough to pass as human. I thought she might even have to send word to her friends that she was not going to be able to join them at the Northern Settlement," Themis muses along with Abrahm.

"Are you ever going to explain what Cleo did to me?" Zoya breaks in, her voice sharp with suppressed anger. "I still can't go anywhere near her without feeling like I want to crawl away."

"She unknowingly used her telepathic control on you," Abrahm said. "She wasn't aware of it, but I will talk to her about it tomorrow when she comes to the lesson. I can get her to reverse it, but I do need you there for the first part of the lesson. She needs to have access to you."

"Sounds good," Zoya assents, stretching and curling up on the ground for a chance to sleep a little bit. She hadn't been involved in many of their conversations about the lessons and didn't seem all that interested in learning more. Themis turns away from her.

"Do you have any ideas on how to better gain control of my suddenly sprouting my coat every time I get distracted?" he asks Abrahm, looking over his currently bare arms that threatened to pop out with fur at any moment.

"It just takes practice. It needs to be a part of your transformation between the Lycan form and the human one." Abrahm motions for him to step back a little way. "As you transform, you allow your fur to come out and thicken." He transforms before Themis's eyes, his dark, gray-streaked fur sprouting long all over his body. As he turns back to human again, the fur recedes. "You need to make the pulling of the hair back into your skin a part of that transformation and get into regular practice with it."

He motions for Themis to try and Themis rolls his neck in his accustomed signal to his body to begin the transformation. The motion wasn't a requirement for him to transform, but Themis had just picked up the trick over the years to allow him to more smoothly transform when he wasn't in danger. Sometimes he just enjoyed the feel of being a Lycan and being able to hunt without the human contrivances. He had learned the trick from one of his buddies in their training courses and it had stuck. Now it was simply habit. As he transforms, he feels the prickly feeling of the hair sprouting long all over his body as he bends forward to rest his weight on his forepaws. His back legs prepare to launch forward, all muscles tense. As he wills himself back to his human frame, he adds the notion of pulling the fur in along his body and he is surprised to find the fur obeying his directive as he stands straight once more in front of Abrahm. The conscious effort of keeping the fur under his skin works.

He stares at the older Alpha in astonishment. "Wow! I'm furless! That feels so much better."

"Each time you transform, it will get easier," Abrahm assures him, glancing over at Zoya dozing by a nearby tree. "Zoya could do it too, if she tried."

"I'm sure I could." Zoya's irritated voice comes muffled from under her arm where her head rests. "But I'm not in the mood to try now. Leave me alone."

Both Alphas chuckle quietly at the form lying against the trees and then move off to continue to work on some other skills Abrahm had talked to him about.

The next evening after having walked and scouted ahead of the humans, Themis and Zoya settle their small camp and prepare for Cleo to come. They know she is aware of where they had set up camp and it takes only about twenty minutes for her to find them.

"What are we learning today?" she asks, her knife at her belt since the other weapons she usually carries are back at camp. She seems a little wary of the other Lycans, especially with Zoya lurking around the edge of the campsite.

"The first thing I need you to do is release the telepathic control you have over Zoya," Abrahm says, glaring at the lurking Beta. "She's currently feeling a little on edge and flighty because she can't be in your presence. You must have ordered her to leave you alone when you were really angry with me and Themis."

"Telepathic control?" Cleo asks, confusion plain on her face. "I don't have the ability to control people. Otherwise I wouldn't need to use my weapons or argue with my friends."

"Do you feel like you have a shudder running up and down your spine?" Abrahm questions her. "For me it's like a warm shudder running down my spine when I send out my control. I imagine it probably feels different to every Alpha, but it might be similar, seeing as we come from the same bloodline."

"I am feeling a shudder down my spine." Cleo nods, giving way to the shiver. "It gets worse when I look at Zoya. How do I get rid of it?"

"Focus on the order you gave her," Abrahm instructs, and Cleo turns in Zoya's direction and closes her eyes. "Now, feel that order fall away. I usually imagine myself cutting a string or pulling a bow apart to give me something physical to picture to make it easier." Cleo seems to shudder, then sigh and relax as if in relief. Zoya too stops pacing and straightens, looking much more at ease.

"Everyone feeling a little bit better?" Abrahm asks, looking over the three faces in front of him. Cleo opens her eyes and nods along with Themis and Zoya. "Good, now I think we should look at that mental control. Zoya, would you be able to stay and help us?" At the look of alarm and dubious contempt on her face, Abrahm grins. "I promise we won't make you do anything stupid. It is only as a means of practicing. I would like Themis to become proficient at the skill as well so we will be better equipped if a band of Omegas decides to come prowling again."

Reluctantly, Zoya steps forward next to Abrahm and the lesson begins. Themis and Cleo take turns trying to order Zoya to do various small tasks, usually picking up twigs or rocks. It only takes Cleo three tries to succeed on her fourth attempt of directing Zoya to pick up a brick near her left foot. Zoya said flatly no, but despite her words, her body moved to bend and lift the brick. As soon as Cleo cut the line of control, Zoya chucked the brick away from herself, startled.

Themis on the other hand struggled. It took several individualized coaching instructions from both Abrahm and Cleo before Themis succeeded in forcing Zoya to bend down and scrawl an X in the dirt at her feet with a stick. With this success, Abrahm suggests a break. Themis and Cleo chat and drink from their waterskins. Zoya rolls the cracks and kinks from her joints in response to her fighting with her own body against the mental control that Cleo and now Themis were exerting on her.

"It's just a bizarre feeling," she complains as they take their break. "It's like I know what I want to do, but there is something inside me that has the wheel and I can do nothing but sit back and watch as they pull and push me around however they want."

Abrahm nods. "I think we can finish our lesson here for now. Give Zoya the chance to get back to feeling in control again." He tries to achieve a sense of what Cleo is feeling. "I think that if we have any problems with Omegas in the future, we won't need to worry. Cleo has a nice handle on her mental control and Themis has made a large step in the right direction. Have a nice evening with your friends, Cleo, and remember that you can just continue to follow this highway pretty much the rest of the way. If you need any more guidance, don't hesitate to ask for directions. But the road should take you straight to one of the entrance points into the settlement."

"Thank you, Abrahm," Cleo says, standing and moving toward the human camp. "I will talk with my friends tonight about the rest of the way. We shouldn't be more than six days away now, should we?"

"I think there are fewer days than that," Abrahm responds. "Just keep going. You'll see the Settlement boundaries a long way before you reach them. They are hard to miss."

And with that, Cleo disappears into the trees. Themis wonders if Abrahm can see the slight thinning of Cleo's face like he had seen. She is getting thinner, despite hunting for her friends. Themis wonders if she ever takes a few of the rabbits she catches and eats them herself or struggles to eat the food her friends cook. He isn't sure, and he thinks about it as he curls up and drifts off to sleep.

CHAPTER SEVEN

In the four days since Cleo arrived, panting and excited to have finally caught up with them, Mandi sits at the fire, watching their fearless leader as she settles her gear in her pack and lays out her sleeping bag before turning toward the fire.

"I'm going to go lay out some snares," Cleo says, standing up and tucking a tiny little knife into her belt. "I'll be back in a few hours. I want to get an idea of the lay of the land and give my snares some time to catch something."

"Sounds good," Elijah says in response. "Just be safe and whistle if you need anything." He watches her go with a grin and turns back to his fire building.

A few minutes later, Mandi stands from her perch on a nearby rock and follows Cleo's clear trail a little way. Once in between the trees, the trail becomes harder to follow, but Mandi is certain of her tracking skills and continues in the direction she is sure Cleo had gone. She follows this trail almost ten minutes before she hears a rustling in the trees behind her and she jumps around, pulling a dagger from her belt, only to come face to face with a rather irate Cleo.

"What are you doing here, Mandi?" she demands, her voice straining to remain calm. "I thought I told you all that I was going to set snares. I don't need you following me a few minutes behind and scaring off all the small critters."

Mandi is stunned to the point of speechlessness at the imposing figure of her friend. When she finally finds her tongue again, she simply states, "I wanted to see if I could help you at all."

"I don't need your help." Cleo's words are short, clipped. "Go back to camp. I'll be back in a few hours." And with that, Cleo stalks off in another direction, away from Mandi and camp. It takes a minute before Mandi can move and she sighs in relief as she begins her short trek back toward the smoky smell of the now lit campfire. *What the hell is she doing?* Mandi demands of herself when she sits back on her boulder seat she had occupied earlier. She sees her friends' smirking faces and shoots them nasty looks.

"Tried to follow her, did you?" Charlie asks, the smirk plain on his face and he looks in the direction of his sister's disappearance. "How long did it take her to spot you and sneak up on you again? Five minutes, maybe ten? Cleo's the best tracker. She can hear you coming a mile away."

"Thanks for the information, oh, snarky one," Mandi snaps back. "But you can't tell me you both aren't even the littlest bit curious about where she's going. What do you think she's actually up to? There's no way she's just setting up snares and waiting for them to catch things, is there?"

"How would you know, miss? I've never walked more than a mile away from the territory in my life before I decided to join my friends on a crusade I think is pointless and stupid!" Elijah crows to shut her up. "Have you ever set up snares? Have you ever sat so still in the woods that animals will walk right past you without realizing you are there?" At Mandi's wordless expression of anger and resentment, he continues. "No? I didn't think so. Cleo has been doing it for years. She knows how to get food even if it seems that there's no food available. So, shut up about wondering what Cleo is doing and get busy with your chores. I would like to make some stew for dinner. Hopefully, Cleo brings us a few rabbits or squirrels." And with that, Elijah turns to continue building the fire and working around the campsite.

Mandi turns without another word to pull out their stew pot and goes digging in everyone's packs for any of the vegetables left from one of the overgrown gardens they had passed the day before. She wants to add as many carrots and other vegetables to the pot to give the stew some varied flavors. Then she grabs some of the waterskins and goes in search of a creek to fill them and the cook pot.

By the time Cleo walks back into camp with two squirrels and a pair of rabbits slung over her shoulders, the pot of water is boiling, ready for the meat and other ingredients to make a good stew.

Mandi pays attention to her leader and quickly notices that, while she has a bowl in front of her filled with stew, all Cleo seems to be doing with the food is push it around and asking questions of the others to distract them. Mandi watches her all through dinner until Charlie stands up.

"I'll take first watch," he says and moves further away from the fire to avoid being night blind when dark falls in less than an hour. Mandi watches as Cleo stands as well and turns away from the fire. Cleo seems to head to her tent with her still full bowl of stew, but Mandi blinks and suddenly, an empty bowl sits outside of the tent where Cleo had ducked underneath the flap.

She's not eating, the nagging voice in her head grumbles as Mandi leans against a tree trunk. *Why isn't she eating? She's getting thinner and it looks like she's just ignoring her own needs right now. Is she just worried about us making it to the settlement up north, or is this a remnant of the illness that had kept her from traveling with us for two days?* Mandi's mind runs through several scenarios, debating each one and trying to decide which one could possibly be at all true.

Over the next two days, Mandi watches Cleo closely for signs of any problems that she is facing. During the first day Cleo seems fine. She takes lead the first day and tail the second. She is attentive, ensuring that everyone drinks well and chews on the strips of deer jerky that keep them nourished through the trip. Mandi notices that Cleo is never seen eating her jerky but thinks that maybe she is just hiding when she eats, or else ripping the strips of jerky into pieces that she can pop into her mouth as needed for something to chew on. Either way, Cleo never shows signs of having problems when they were walking.

When they stop, Cleo always helps them unpack, then tells them she is going to go set snares. The first night she goes out toward the west. The second time, toward the south. Both times, Mandi watches her go with the same fascination and suspicion, knowing full well that Cleo is keeping something from them.

Cleo returns from her trips after two to three hours looking a little red in the face or else breathing a little harder than she did after their walks during the day, but there are two or three little animals gutted and strung over one or both of her shoulders. *Well, she's good at hiding whatever it is she's hiding,* Mandi concedes as they all settle down for food and a little rest before the next day's six-hour hike. At this rate, they should be coming close to the territory and Mandi would be happy not to be living as a nomad anymore.

While everyone in the camp is now asleep or settled into the watch, a small shower of meteors shimmers across the sky.

*   *   *

"It's too risky!" Abrahm argues for what seems like the dozenth time that day. "You shouldn't go anywhere near the Northern Settlement. You don't have the control you need yet to be able to pass through their security without getting spotted yet. If they find out you're Lycan, you'll be killed on sight! They've shot at me before and they didn't have a good look at me!"

"I've been able to fool my friends for the last several days. I think I can pass whatever security is set up in the settlement," Cleo argues back, her face set stubbornly. "I brought my friends this far. I can get them and me across the border into the settlement too. I know I can."

"But can you ensure that you won't become a body on the edge of the settlement?" Abrahm argues back, just as stubborn as his daughter. "I don't want to even think about what they would do to you if they found out you are Lycan. If you're lucky, they'll shoot you on sight. If not, they may torture you or even experiment on you since you can transform into a human. They may want to use you to study Lycan powers. They can't get a hold of you!"

Abrahm's worry, while completely valid for the reasons he explained several times already to Cleo, is twofold. On the one hand, he knows full well that Cleo is one of the most adept Lycans he's ever seen transforming into a human form. She doesn't even look different from how she looked before the bite. She could most certainly pass through any security they tried on her, but he couldn't tell how long that control could last. The second part of his worry is that he knows Cleo is slipping. He has noticed for two days she has been losing weight and becoming more and more skeletal. He is worried that she has stopped eating and might at some point start snapping at her friends in her hunger-crazed state. He knows that she is playing a risky game now. If she goes much longer without food, he knows that she will start to look at her friends as a source of food and that is the last thing Abrahm wants.

"I don't care," Cleo huffs. "I am going to the Northern Settlement and that is final. I am going to go there; I am going to settle down there and I am going to live a completely normal life." The way she says it so matter-of-factly makes him want to sob. He lets out a snort of irritation and suppressed emotion.

"Cleo." Themis's voice is low, breaking into the stalemate between father and daughter. "Come on. Let's go get some water and a bit of air. I want to talk to you."

Abrahm watches as Cleo reluctantly follows at Themis's insistent tugging at her arm. Themis is a good man, strong, loyal, dependable. He knows how to work with people and get others to follow along with most of what he says. Abrahm gazes after them, wondering if there is something between the two young Alphas but decides not to pursue the question. Zoya pops up beside him and her voice startles him out of his thoughts.

"They look cute together, don't they?" she asks, looking after her leader and the young woman, both walking close to each other as they duck between trees and under limbs. "Of course, I've always been kind of hoping that he'd take me as his mate." Her words are casual, as if discussing the weather for the next day. "I've never fully offered myself to him, but I never flinched away while we worked together. I was always there if he needed comfort or anything else from me."

"I'm sure he appreciated it," Abrahm sighs, rolling his eyes. "Most Alphas mate because of a specific pull toward an individual. They sense the strength and potential that a mate brings and decide based on how much potential there is that a strong offspring will be born. He probably didn't pick you because he knew that you two would be working and traveling together. You weren't stable or able to raise a baby at the time."

"Thanks." Zoya scoffs. "That makes me feel really special." He sees out of the corner of his eye Zoya rolling her own skyward. He chuckles.

"Let's get settled. I'm hoping that he talks to her and they have a decent conversation. I also hope he feeds her." Abrahm spots Zoya's glance at him that confirms that she has noticed too. "I don't think she's been eating herself since we told her what she is. I think she's ashamed of herself and that self-loathing is beginning to manifest in self-destructive behaviors. If she continues to refuse to eat, she will be putting her friends and herself in great danger."

Zoya nods in understanding and Abrahm turns to a nearby tree. He curls up in the bowl of the roots and makes himself comfortable, keeping an ear out in the direction of Themis and Cleo. He can hear the murmur of voices but cannot make out the words distinctly. He lets himself sleep for a while, not really paying attention to what is happening, but after just over an hour, he hears raised voices coming from Themis and Cleo.

They are arguing, fighting about something Abrahm has missed. Now that he is paying attention, all he hears is Cleo's voice, loud and full of power, yelling at Themis.

"Go away! Leave me alone!" Abrahm feels a shudder go up his spine at the sheer might of power and control in the voice before he hears Cleo dash off into the trees. He hears Themis struggling through the brambles and branches, as if unable to walk properly— Abrahm guesses that Cleo has hit him. When he stumbles into their clearing a few long minutes later, he seems unharmed but severely shaken and unfocused. Abrahm recognizes the symptoms of someone under the control of an Alpha but is confused at how this could have happened. Normal Alphas have control over the other variants of Lycans but never other Alphas. They are all so evenly matched in power and abilities that no Alphas can feasibly control each other. That is the reason there are different territories. Different Alphas disagree on policies, so they split off to make their own territories in different areas. Those that disagree with everyone's policies are usually the roaming Alphas.

But to have an Alpha that can control other Alphas, that is something new, something unheard of.

"Which way did she go?" Abrahm asks Themis as he stumbles into the tree. He points vaguely in the eastern direction and Abrahm is off, using his senses of smell and hearing to guide him to the lost, scared Alpha.

When he gets close enough, he hears her sobs and slows his pace. He walks slowly and easily toward her, careful to be deliberate about his movements. He doesn't want to set her off if he can help it. She seems to hear him, her sobs lessen, and she hiccups herself into a more coherent state before turning to face him.

"What do you want?" she demands, her brows creased with suppressed anger over puffy, red-rimmed eyes and a running nose. "Why can't you just leave me alone?"

"I'm your father," Abrahm replies. "I'm just looking out for you. It's my job to protect you, even if I'm protecting you from yourself." He moves slowly, moving every so often so that he gets nearer and nearer to her. "Themis made it back to us. He's under your control, like Zoya was."

This startles Cleo who looks up at him in shock. "What? But I thought we couldn't control each other!" Her voice cracks and squeaks from the sobs. Abrahm holds out a hand in peace indicating she should stay sitting.

"I didn't think it was possible," he says to her, moving closer again. "But you are proving just how special you are."

Cleo glares at him. "This is all your fault!" she hurls at him. "Why did you fall for my mother? Why couldn't you have been my brother's father? Why do I have to be this beast?" Her words cut at Abrahm and indicate just how poorly Cleo is coping with her newfound situation. "I was perfectly happy being ignorant of who, no, of what I am! Now I'm a danger to my friends. I should never have brought them on this journey! Kiya's dead, I'm a monster, Charlie and Elijah are worried about me, and Mandi keeps trying to get us all to turn around and go back! Why do I bother keeping going? We're all going to die soon anyway. What does it matter?" Cleo sobs, burying her face in her arms and curling up on herself.

Abrahm steps forward to embrace his daughter, but it is as if she senses his movement and she immediately lashes out, not only with her arm to stop him physically but with her mental control. She silently orders him to stop, to freeze, and for the briefest of heartbeats, they stand there frozen. Then the instant passes and Cleo is staring blankly at her father, unable to understand what had just happened.

"You're a Master," Abrahm murmurs, hardly audible. Cleo doesn't look at him but instead turns and immediately flees, darting into the trees.

CHAPTER EIGHT

You're a monster and now no one can stop you, the voice in Cleo's head snarls at her, biting and snapping to have free reign over her actions. *You should just kill yourself and get it over with! No one will mourn you, and your friends can get on with their journey.* "I'm just as worth saving as the others," she argues back with herself, but even she doesn't believe what she says. Despite everyone's checking, she has been able to evade everyone's questions and has slowly been starving herself. Each day that goes by her stomach growls even more, but she is able to simply ignore the gnawing pangs from lack of food. Each time she hunts, she has the urge to scarf down the flesh of the small creatures she catches, but to her more human side, the sight of the raw meat just makes her sick. She's fighting herself just for the right to live and be able to be her own person.

If Elijah and Charlie knew what you are, they'd put a quarrel or an arrow through your heart faster than you could spit, the nagging voice continues and Cleo dashes away as if she can outrun the voice and her racing thoughts. She climbs a nearby hill and finds a sheltered cave that blocks her from view of anyone.

She sits against the wall furthest from the cave opening, crossing her legs, and closing her eyes. She takes several deep breaths, pulling on every ounce of strength and perseverance to clear her mind and pull up an internal image of her mother.

When she opens her eyes, she holds the image of her mother in her heart and before her sits a woman slightly shorter than she is with straight auburn hair, almost the same color as Cleo's with a similar face shape and the same long, straight nose.

"Hi, Mom," Cleo half cries, hardly able to keep herself calm. The woman smiles at her and Cleo gives a watery grin back. "I miss you. So does Charlie, though he won't admit it."

"I know, darling." Cleo's mother's voice sounds similar to Cleo's with the same lilts on certain letters. "But I'm not here to talk about Charlie. I'm here to talk about you. What are you worrying about, my little warrior?"

"Did you know Abrahm was a Lycan?" Cleo bursts out when her mother finishes the question. "I mean, did he ever tell you what he was or were you just so smitten with him that you didn't see that he wasn't human?"

"I didn't know your father was anything other than a human," her mother replies, her voice echoed and distant. "I fell in love with him just because he seemed like a nice man. He was handsome, smart, funny, easy to talk to. I had been looking for someone to live with and start a family with. He was in our community for a few days and we connected. I fell for him and we had a few nights together where nothing else mattered. And then he left, and I never saw him again. I married Charlie's father not a month later and had you. I was never sure if you were his or Abrahm's, but part of me hoped that you were Abrahm's just to have a little bit of him to keep as a reminder."

"So, you suspected I might not be Dad's kid?" Cleo demands, anger flaring in her eyes. "Why didn't you tell me there was a possibility that I wasn't my father's daughter?"

"I wasn't sure." Her mother looks apologetic. "I wanted you to have as normal a life as you could, given how crazy our world is right now."

"Well, my normal life has just been thrown into the worst kind of chaos and there is nothing you or I can do to fix it." Cleo's eyes are filled with tears. "I don't want to keep going! I want you back, I want to be back with you and Dad and Charlie in the Nashville Settlement, and I want to go back to the way things were. I don't want to be a Lycan, I don't want to be Abrahm's daughter and I'm not even sure I want to keep living anymore!"

On her last word, she bursts into hysterical sobs and cannot get a hold of herself. She curls up on the ground and cries. She cries for the family and friends she left behind in Nashville. She cries for the brother she has a connection to. She sobs for the life she might have had if her mother hadn't been killed by Lycans. She sobs for the loss of her human life that she can never go back to now that she has been bitten.

Her sobs go on and on, finally petering out into huge wracking deep breaths. She gasps and continues to try and master herself, but each time she tries to keep her head, another image of a part of her old life floats before her eyes. She cannot escape the fact that, despite her pretending that everything is fine, she hasn't eaten since the first lesson from Abrahm seven days ago. Each time she smells the food her friends make she feels the overwhelming urge to vomit. When she makes a kill or hunts one of the bigger animals, she gets the urge to rip into the flesh of the creature and that sickens her too.

"What do I do now, Mom?" Cleo glances up at the shade of her mother in a desperate plea. "I can't keep going on like this, can I?"

"No." Her mother shakes her head. "You will be putting your friends in danger if you keep going without food. Soon they will start to look appealing to you and you might accidentally try to take a bite out of them instead of the animals you hunt."

Cleo doesn't want to admit it to herself, but she has already had the strong urge to bite and kill each of her human friends. It had already happened when Mandi tried to follow her.

Cleo had not been paying attention at first, moving quickly and almost soundlessly through the trees as she thought about what Abrahm would teach her today. Then the sound of cracking branches and rustling leaves had piqued her interest. She had taken a small sniff of the air and had caught Mandi's scent following her trail. Cleo hadn't planned on doubling back, but her body had acted of its own accord, circling around the fumbling human with hardly a sound. By the time Cleo had realized she was inches away from Mandi, she had grabbed control of herself and had spooked Mandi instead. She had simply sent the girl scuttling back to camp, but it could have been so much worse.

Cleo shudders, blocking out the other memories of her friends trying to follow her into the woods after she'd told them she was snaring rabbits.

"It's already almost happened three times," Cleo admits aloud. "I don't want to risk it happening again, but I don't know what else to do. I can't eat the meat right off the carcass. It's too disgusting to think about. I don't want to become the monster. I won't lose control of it."

"Just allowing yourself to change form doesn't mean you are becoming the monster you think you might be," Cleo's mother says softly. "As long as you can continue to feel like yourself, you won't lose control to the wolfish side of yourself. You will still be able to change back to a human. You heard what Abrahm said. You don't look abnormal for a human. You should be able to pass any inspection. You instinctively changed yourself into the form you were most familiar with and that is your human one. You won't lose that just by transforming once and a while to eat."

"No!" Cleo protests, turning away from her mother's shade. "I won't do it! I won't let myself change into the monster. I hate Lycans. You of all people should know that. They are the reason you're dead!"

"They are also the reason you're still alive," Cleo's mother argues back. "Zoya and Themis tried to prevent the Omegas from overrunning you and your friends while you slept. They are the reason that you, Charlie, Elijah, and Mandi made it out. You have made yourself a stereotype that doesn't fit every Lycan just like most stereotypes don't fit the majority of people they are about. You think that all Lycans are just like the creatures that killed me and attacked our settlement. According to Abrahm, Themis, and Zoya, there are different kinds of Lycans just like there are different kinds of people. You hate Omegas and apparently you are not alone in that hatred. It seems that most people, Lycan and human, hate Omegas. They are the lowest of the low. But you are not one of them. Keep that in mind."

"But what if I become like them?" Cleo whimpers, covering her face with her hands. "I can't let myself transform or I risk becoming just like them."

"No, you won't," a male's voice interrupts Cleo's internal fight and she looks up, startled. "You won't change, and that's a promise." Themis stands in the entrance of the cave, his arms raised, palms out, with a bag slung across his chest.

*   *   *

"I'm worried about her." Abrahm paces their camp after Cleo has stormed off. "She's going to end up hurting someone if she's not careful. Either that or she'll starve herself to death. She should be gaining weight if anything, considering she's been catching more meat than normal for her friends."

"I know she hasn't been eating," Themis interrupts before Abrahm can continue his rambling worries. "Now, I'm going to go after her. She's probably getting herself so worked up about everything that has happened today already. I don't need her to do something she'll regret later, just to feel normal now."

And without another glance back at Abrahm or Zoya lurking in the background, Themis disappears. He can sense where the humans are and can tell that Cleo didn't go back to her friends. He knows that she won't return to her human friends unless she is one hundred percent in control of her emotions and powers, and right now he knows that she is feeling about the furthest thing possible from control. He catches the vaguest suggestion of her scent as he moves around the humans' camp. He smells a deer nearby and considers its scent for a moment. It doesn't seem to be moving quickly, and it is upwind from him.

He hesitates only briefly before turning toward the scent of prey, deciding that if he was going to find Cleo, he would need to try and get her to eat. The best way to do that would be to get a rather large animal and bring her steaks of the meat instead of the carcasses. His judgments about the deer are correct and he is able to sneak to within about a yard of the buck before it catches the scent of him and by that point it is too late. He kills it with a swift bite to the throat and a violent shake of the head to snap the neck.

With the taste of blood in his mouth, Themis has to struggle against his instincts to rip into the body himself, but instead pulls the hated knife from his belt and begins to systematically gut and slice off a few steaks from the main parts of the carcass. He can master his animal instincts until he has almost ten large steaks cut away from the body in front of him and placed in a leather sack slung across his torso. He leaves the deer, trusting it to the wandering packs of dogs to take care of the remaining carcass.

With his prizes securely slung and exerting a significant pull on his left shoulder, he moves off in search of more difficult prey.

He catches the briefest whiffs of Cleo and follows his nose until he reaches the point where he can't sense Abrahm, Zoya, or the humans. He looks around and sees a large area pockmarked with what looks like several dozen holes of varying sizes and depths. He inhales deeply and catches his first strong scent of Cleo. The wind whips around him briefly and he thinks he hears faint shouting nearby, but with the shift of the wind again, the sound disappears. The scent of Cleo, however, is a better indication of where she huddles. Pricking his ears, he also hears speaking.

It is Cleo's voice. "No!" she says as he moves closer to the smell and sound. "I won't do it! I won't let myself change into the monster. I hate Lycans. You of all people should know that. They are the reason you're dead!"

Cleo's voice stops and Themis moves forward, finding the cave. Inside, barely visible in the gloomy half-light, he spots the seated figure of Cleo, glaring fixedly at the opposite side of the wall.

"But what if I become like them?" Cleo whimpers, covering her face with her hands. "I can't let myself transform or I risk becoming just like them."

"No, you won't." Themis takes a deep breath and moves forward, into Cleo's line of sight. "You won't change, and that's a promise." He holds his hands up, palms out to show that he means no harm and kneels about two yards away from her. Cleo looks at him, as if not fully believing her eyes;

it's as if she's expecting him to vanish into thin air before her. Themis sees her nostrils flare as she catches the scent of blood from the bag on his shoulder and then watches as she half flinches away, half moves toward the scent.

"I can help you, if you'll let me try," he offers, pulling the bag from his shoulders and opening it. "I brought some raw meat. I thought it might be easier than a rabbit or a fox. All I have are raw steaks here. No other body parts."

Cleo flinches away from the meat. "I can't. I can't eat cooked meat. It makes me sick and I'm already so hungry. I fear I might make myself even worse at controlling myself if I eat anything."

"I'm not planning on cooking the meat." Themis scoffs, cracking his neck in anticipation of transformation for food. "We can't eat cooked meat. We need to eat it raw, but most of the time, we eat in our transformed states. Our teeth are better made for ripping into flesh and it helps us feel slightly less human when we eat as our Lycan forms. It lessens the burden on us a little bit."

"But I can't transform!" Cleo's face is horror stricken. "If I transform, I might not be able to change back. I'll be stuck as a beast forever! I won't ever be able to see my friends again; I'll be an outcast forever. I will never be able to live a normal life!"

Themis ignores the risk of scaring her in his determination to comfort her. He knows how difficult it is to no longer be in control of yourself. He has been feeling that way for so long before Abrahm's valuable coaching.

Themis wraps his arms around Cleo and pulls her close, giving her something physical to hold on to in what must seem like a swirling maelstrom of chaotic emotions and impossible choices. At Themis's touch, Cleo's tenuous hold on her control breaks and she bursts into renewed sobs. This time, the sobs are rawer, more emotion-filled than they had been before. It is a real relief to hold onto someone who has been or is going through something similar.

"I will help you through anything you need me to," Themis murmurs into her hair as he holds her. "We can go step by step. One thing at a time. I just need you to be able to trust me and know that I can help you get through any of these challenges." He strokes her hair, muttering soothing words to her just to keep her calm. As he continues to mutter nonsense in her ear and smooth her bedraggled hair down and away from her face, she slowly softens and becomes calmer and more collected. She even goes so far as to pull away slightly to wipe at her eyes and nose, smearing tears and snot across her face. Themis hands her a small cloth.

"Now that we've covered the basics and you have now realized that I am here to help you, we can move on to step one. We need to make sure you are capable of changing back into your human form."

Cleo glances up at his face, worry in her eyes. "Are you sure this is a good idea? What if I can't get myself to change back? What if I'm stuck forever—" Before she can continue to ramble and get herself worked up, Themis interrupts.

"We'll just start off with changing for a minute and immediately changing back." He says, reaching out his hands to her. She takes them shyly. "We'll hold hands so that I can guide you between your forms. It makes it easier to follow someone's lead before you try to transform on your own."

He rolls his head and feels his transformation come on. He also feels Cleo across from him, shrugging her own shoulders and beginning to change in turn. He feels the slightly delayed timing in her change, her arms lengthening a few seconds behind the lengthening of his own. He also notices the continued hesitation in her transformation. He nudges her with encouragement, pushing his own transformation to completion and waiting for her to finish. She does so and sits shuddering in her Lycan form, gazing down at her hands and legs beneath her.

Themis can't help but appreciate the beauty of her form. She is lean, tall, gracefully built with a light covering of auburn fur all over her body. Despite her apparent fear of being in her Lycan form, she has the posture and possesses distinct impression of power and authority that comes from being an Alpha. Her eyes, while a sharp gray as a human, are now a brilliant blue-gray more keen and commanding. He lets his tongue loll out of the right side of his mouth and tilts his head in a wolf grin and she almost involuntarily lets out a bark of laughter at the sight.

At his nudge, Cleo starts to try and transform back to her human self. This time, Themis allows her to try alone, figuring out her own ways of triggering her transformation. He nods in encouragement when he watches her toss her head back and sigh long and low. With the exhale, her transformation begins. Themis follows her, easing himself back into his human form. While connected to her by touch, he can draw from her experience of what being human means and finds himself mimicking some of what she has felt. When Cleo glances up at him with her human face, a start of surprise makes him cock his head.

"What's the matter?" he asks, looking at her with concern. "What is it?"

"You don't look the same as you did before you changed," she whispers, awed. "I wish you could see yourself. You look completely human. Before you had slightly too broad shoulders and your arms and legs were slightly too long for the rest of your body, but now, you are humanly proportioned. Did I do something?"

"You might have." Themis looks down at his frame in puzzlement. "I've never transformed while touching someone else or in the same way we just did. I've only ever learned to transform on my own. That was just how it was done. I only tried to guide you to make sure you knew you weren't alone."

"Well, I feel a little better," Cleo murmurs. "Do we need to change again?"

"It will make eating a little bit easier for you, at least for a while." Themis nods and reaches out for her hands. "If you need to go slow, we can do that. I am just here to help you get through the worry about eating the raw meat."

Cleo takes his hands and together they both shift into their Lycan forms again. Cleo's transformation feels smoother than it did the first time and Themis doesn't sense the hesitation that had been present when he first guided her into the transformation.

"How do you feel?" he asks, admiring her profile as a fully transformed Lycan. *"You look good. You don't look nearly as frightened as you did before."*

"I feel okay." Cleo's response is timid, but her voice is steady despite the unfamiliar growl that she makes because her Lycan muzzle can't move around the human syllables. *"I don't think I'll ever become fully used to being in this form, but I don't mind it right now."*

Themis chuckles through his own muzzle, almost laughing harder at how strange it feels laughing as a Lycan. He hadn't done that since he was a young boy playing with his pack mates. He shakes his head and turns to the bag.

"Let's try one steak each for now and we can see how you feel after the first one," he suggests, pulling two of the deer steaks from the pack and handing one to Cleo. Almost as soon as she puts a paw on the steak, she rips into it with a ferocity Themis didn't expect. She gets through the first half of the chunk of meat before she seems to realize what she is doing, and she balks. The look of disgust flits across her face and Themis moves closer to her.

"I just feel disgusting," she murmurs, still holding the flesh in her hands. *"But it smells so good. And honestly, it tastes good. That's what freaks me out so much. It just seems so wrong!"* She tries to look away from the bloody chunk in her paws, but can't seem to manage to drop it, despite her words.

Themis nudges her gently and takes an exaggerated bite of his own meat, savoring the flavor before swallowing. *"It only feels wrong to the human side of your brain. Let the Lycan side loose for a bit. You'll still be able to collar it later. I'll help, I promise.*

Just like I helped you change last time; I'll be here to help keep your wolfish side in check."

Cleo leans unconsciously into his nudge and takes a deep breath before continuing to devour the meat. Her stomach lets out a loud grumble as she finishes the first serving. He grins and pulls a second serving out for her, smiling at the sight of her eating with him. He pulls his own second steak out from the bag and finishes it at about the same time as Cleo.

"I think I'm done, for now," she rumbles, licking the blood from her paws. Themis leans forward and licks at her muzzle, cleaning the remnants of blood and deer meat from her face in long strokes of his tongue. She stays still through his ministrations until he finishes, and then moves forward when he stops to return the favor. When she manages to clean the last of the blood from his face, he takes her paws and again they transform back into their human forms.

Worry begins to seep into her mind slightly, realizing this is the first time that she's eaten in a while.

"Won't I get sick?" she asks, looking up at Themis's face. He grins down at her.

"We're different from humans," he replies, brushing his hand against her cheek to soothe her. "You might have gone crazy if you hadn't eaten for longer, but meat won't make you sick. You get your strength from the food you eat."

Cleo smiles and leans her head into his hand. They stand close together, barely breathing, barely moving for what seems like forever before Cleo flinches and whirls for the entrance to the cave.

"Charlie!" she cries, alarmed. "He's coming, looking for me! He'll see you!" Her terror momentarily blinds her, and she paces back to him and then to the entrance. She seems torn between two desires, the desire to stay with Themis and the desire to go to her brother's calls.

"We'll say that I'm from the human settlement where you stayed to get over the 'fever' from the Omega scratch," Themis suggests off the top of his head. "I'm just checking that you're doing okay and was bringing food to you." He holds up the bag of deer meat, looking rueful. "I was going to bring some of the meat to Abrahm and Zoya, but I'm sure you four will have better uses for it. Try to keep some of the raw meat separate so you can eat it as you go," he suggests, and together they walk out of the cave.

*   *   *

Charlie paces restlessly around camp as the sun sets. *She should be back by now.* He thinks about the last week or so since Cleo has returned from the mysterious settlement, fully healed from an infection she received from a scratch during their fight with the Lycans. *She's been getting thinner and thinner. What if she got into a fight with something and she's lying somewhere in the forest, dying? What if she's been getting weaker from a slower acting infection that the other settlement didn't catch?* All these scenarios and more play inside his head as it becomes later and later. Finally, he stands.

"I'm going to go look for her," he says to Mandi, sitting by the fire she stokes. Elijah looks up from where he is preparing a rabbit. "She should have been back by now. I just want to make sure she's okay."

The other two don't argue but continue what they are doing. Charlie knows that Elijah is nervous, but still he keeps busy with his work so that he doesn't start pacing and go off looking for her himself. *Elijah's a good man; Cleo's lucky to have someone as devoted as he is.*

But Cleo hasn't been around enough to see just how devoted Elijah is. In fact, Cleo is barely around or conscious of anything going on in camp anymore. Charlie has noticed that she is participating in fewer discussions of which direction they need to head in or what roads to take. During their recent travels, she has been almost silent, only speaking when absolutely necessary to get everyone to go in the right direction, or to let them know about a danger of some sort. It is strange not to hear her joking or jesting with Elijah or Mandi, and even more strange to not have her talking beside him.

Each evening, Cleo has slipped away under the pretense of setting up snares and then to sit and wait for them to catch some prey. Each evening she brings back a rabbit or two, sometimes a bunch of squirrels or other small prey that have wandered into the snares. Charlie watches her carefully when she comes back. She always sits with them as they eat, but now she seems distracted throughout the meal and Charlie is sure she never touches the food in her bowl. Even in a week's time, he can see her face growing narrower and bonier. He isn't sure if she is starting to feel the pressures of getting them from the Nashville Settlement up to the Northern Settlement, or if there was some other strain on her that is causing her to be so distracted, but he was sure that there was a possibility that she might not be able to fight if she comes across even the weakest of Lycans over the course of an evening's scavenging.

So, he grabs his bow and a quiver of arrows, ensures his dagger is strapped to his belt before ducking into the trees. He follows her trail a little way before recognizing that Cleo had crisscrossed her trail so both Lycans and humans have trouble following her. He sighs and begins looking around for likely places where Cleo might have gone.

He spots an open clearing a little way through the trees and heads in that direction. Knowing his sister, she is likely hiding in a cave, keeping herself hidden from her prey and allowing herself to settle against a wall. As he enters the clearing, Charlie is startled to find that there are several different caves surrounding the area. What is more, he hears rustlings coming from several of the different cave openings.

"Cleo!" he calls, looking around. Some of the rustlings stop or become louder before cutting off quickly. "Cleo! Where are you?" From out of one of the caves in front of him, bursts his sister and a stranger. Charlie immediately pulls an arrow from his quiver and nocks his bow at the dark-haired man following Cleo.

"Cleo! Who the hell is that?" he demands as Cleo jumps in front of the arrow. He loosens his grip on the thin projectile.

"Charlie!" Cleo cries, her hands extended. "This is James! He's from the settlement where I went after I got injured. He and his settlement helped me get back on my feet as quickly as I did! It's all thanks to him and his friends!"

James/Themis holds out his hands in supplication. "I just thought I'd catch up to see how Cleo was doing. Make sure there weren't any lingering effects from her injuries."

Charlie reluctantly lowers his bow and allows Cleo to give him a hug. "So, you helped my sister? How did you find us?"

"Cleo said that you were heading up to the Northern Settlement, so I just followed the roads northeast." James's response makes sense. "I figured you all wouldn't travel more than six or seven hours a day, and I know when you left. I took a shorter route, resting when I needed to and was able to travel rather quickly. I saw the smoke of your fire last night and followed you well. Cleo ran into me while she was setting up snares."

"He brought us some deer meat that he hunted today," Cleo pipes up, pulling the heavy-looking satchel from James's shoulder. "We were just heading back to camp. I'm sorry I took so long. My snares were just not catching anything today and I was determined to bring back something fresh for either a late dinner or breakfast in the morning."

Charlie looks at James once more with suspicion before turning to the bag Cleo shoves at him. "You're staying the night?" he asks the stranger. "Or do you already have a campsite set up nearby?"

"I'm not staying," James says quickly. "I just came to see how Cleo was doing. I also figured I would give you the meat, as there are so many more of you. I shot it down as I was coming up on your camp. Now I should start on my way back to my territory. I think I can still get a few hours of travel on my own before I stop to sleep."

Cleo looks at James and Charlie can see a look pass between them that he doesn't like. They seem far too familiar for them to have met just once, and Charlie's concern lies not just for Cleo but for Elijah back at camp. Charlie knows Elijah has been hoping to win Cleo's hand for the last few years. But it seems that this stranger has stolen Cleo's attention. Charlie hopes that James will be gone for good after today so that his friends can get on with their lives. "Good luck with your travels," Charlie says, reaching out for Cleo's hand. "Let's get back. Mandi and Eli are waiting for us. They have dinner ready. We'll have to put some of the venison out to dry as jerky for later." And without looking back, Charlie draws Cleo away.

He waits until they are several yards into the tree before rounding on her. "Are you crazy?!" he yells, clutching at her shoulders and shaking her. "Who the hell was that?! He's a complete stranger! He could have slit your throat and disappeared, and we never would have found you again!"

"Charlie!" Cleo wrenches herself out of her brother's grip and holds out her arms in defense. "I knew who he was! He was one of the people that helped heal me. I believe his story, and I need you to trust me! I don't appreciate you giving me hell about allowing people you don't know anywhere around me! I am fine. I have been having a rough time of things recently and I was able to talk with James like I haven't been able to talk to anyone in a while. I need you to let me keep myself healthy and not run off people who have helped me! I don't need you to protect my virtue any more than you need me to play matchmaker with you now that Kiya is gone!" And without another word or glance, Cleo storms off in the direction of camp.

CHAPTER NINE

"We're almost there!" Mandi's voice sounds excited and relieved as she gazes over the crest of the road at the distant line of defensive walls. She also views soldiers armed with guns and other weaponry. "It looks so close! Do you think we'll reach it by tonight?" She turns to Cleo who walks in front of her.

"No." Cleo's voice is definite. "We've been walking for four hours. Another two might put us within a day's walk of the settlement's borders, but I don't fancy walking up to the gates in the middle of the night. They might shoot us without asking questions. We'll camp in two hours before we get too close, keep the fire low, and in the morning, we'll start walking toward the settlement. We might make it there before midday if we get up early enough." Mandi continues to jabber incessantly beside her, but Cleo decides to ignore her. She has more important problems.

Cleo feels the satchel over her shoulder as well as the bag on her back. The satchel carries the remaining three steaks of meat that she has kept to herself, telling the others she wants to use raw meat to get a wolf or dog in a snare the next time they stop for the night. She knows she needs the meat to keep herself human for as long as possible. She knows she needs to talk with Abrahm, Themis, and Zoya as well, but she isn't sure if she is ready to face the three Lycans.

"Cleo?" Charlie's voice interrupts her thoughts as they begin to turn to the left, the highway winding around large fields covered in brush and growing trees. "Do you want to keep following the road, or should we cut through some of the fields now that we have a pretty good view of where we're heading?" His question is the first time he's spoken to her since the night before and Cleo can sense the awkwardness.

"Let's keep following the road," Cleo says. "I'd like to stay as protected as possible when we camp and if we stay near the road, we might find an overpass or something to camp beneath. It looks like it might storm tonight." She has been watching the sky since they left their camp that morning and the clouds on the eastern horizon have continued to grow darker despite the fairly clear and sunny weather they have enjoyed for weeks. "We might even want to consider getting under some shelter a little bit earlier than we normally do."

They had been lucky enough to only have to walk through three or four days of rain during their almost month-long trip, but had woken up several days to the ground wet and saturated from a late night rain that came and left before dawn. Only the person on third or fourth shift of the watch remembers the rain, having stood in it themselves.

As it turns out, they manage to get their full six hours of walking in before hunkering down under a still-standing overpass. They settle down to camp just as the drizzle begins. Cleo has been pacing near the edge of the overpass, debating with herself about leaving their camp after having set up her own tent and laying out her food supplies to allow Elijah or Mandi use of them for dinner.

"If you're going out, make sure you be careful," Elijah calls at her as he settles about starting a fire with the wood they have collected on their walk. "Don't stay out too late, and if it starts to get really stormy, come back. I think we'll all be pretty safe under here for the night. I don't think we really need a watch."

"I'll be back soon," Cleo promises and ducks out into the persistent drizzle. She heads immediately for where she hears and smells Abrahm, Zoya, and Themis. *I still don't know what to do. They're going to argue with me about going into the settlement. They'll say it's too dangerous for me to go anywhere near the settlement as a Lycan. They'll make the argument that the humans will be able to tell that I'm a Lycan. I've been able to fool my friends for almost two weeks. I think I can fool a couple more people.*

As she gets closer to the Lycan camp, she slows as she continues to argue with herself. *You are strong enough to keep yourself hidden. You'll be able to keep yourself under control and to only eat meat. You could join the hunting team for the settlement and be able to go out on your own to hunt food. You're an excellent hunter and you could be able to find prey that no one else could find or catch. You've proven that you can shoot deer without ruining the meat. You've demonstrated that you can sense prey much further away than humans and even further away than Abrahm and Themis. Your senses will keep you safe and keep you able to blend in. Who knows? You might even begin to be able to stomach cooked meat in time and be able to eat with your friends instead of pretending. But what if you lose control? You can't guarantee that you will be able to eat raw meat but once every couple of days. You were pretty darn close to snapping last time you went on a fast. What if this time you can't control yourself? Themis won't be there to save you.*

I'll save myself, Cleo insists to herself, but she has stopped moving. *I won't need anyone to save me. I'll be able to keep myself calm and after a few days in the settlement, I'll be able to find my way around and find little secluded corners where I can eat my meat without people seeing me.* Cleo looks around herself in sudden realization of where she is and starts walking again. She barely notices that she is moving parallel about halfway between the two camps, pacing without realizing that she is held on a knife's blade of indecision.

People will start to notice even in the first day if you don't eat anything. The little nagging voice is back. *They'll start to notice and start to talk. They won't talk to you, but they'll talk to each other behind your back. You will be watched and stared at in suspicion if you don't eat. I'm sure they will be just as stingy and strict about eating what you are given just like at our first settlement. They will expect you to eat everything you are given, and my guess is that you won't be able to stay with your friends or eat with your friends. You'll be shown into boarding houses where you'll have to make do while they find places for you and your friends to work. You'll have to follow their rules and follow what they tell you when they give you your jobs.*

Then I'll follow the rules, Cleo affirms to herself. *I'll be their perfect soldier. I'll stomach the food they give me, and if I have to, I'll throw it up later. I will ask to be put in a hunting party as soon as I can. I will make myself useful and draw as little attention to myself as possible except for proving that I am worthy of being a hunter.*

Is that why you're out here, stalking between the camps? Waiting for your prey to fall into your lap? Or is it that you are just too scared to face Abrahm and the others, seeing as you've almost completely made up your mind to go against what they think would be best for you? You know they want you to join them as they go back to the territory Zoya and Themis came from. They don't want you going to the humans. You know they are going to throw a fit, and they are going to tell you all the things you are determined either not to see or that you think you can avoid. Who's to say they aren't right?

"I do!" Cleo barks aloud, then looks around to see if anyone heard her. She takes a deep breath and starts off toward the Lycan camp again, determined and ready for the Lycans no matter what they say.

*   *   *

"She'll be in danger from the moment she walks through those walls!" Abrahm rumbles, pacing in front of the view they have of the distant walls of the human settlement. "I don't want her to go anywhere near that place! Even being here makes me nervous! They could come out here and shoot us all dead. They'll know she's not human. They'll capture her and torture her just to try and find out how we work, and then they'll use that information to try and wipe us all out, only to get themselves wiped out in the process!" Abrahm punches at a tree nearby and nearly puts a hole through the trunk. He shakes his hand in pain and to get the tingling of his hand to stop.

"I agree with you," Themis breaks into Abrahm's ranting. "She'll be in danger. But you know she's stubborn. If she's dead set on going with her friends, there's nothing we can do to dissuade her. She's as stubborn as you, if not more. There's no way we can talk her out of something she doesn't want to do, and she is pretty dead set on staying with her friends. She doesn't want to abandon them as they walk into something unfamiliar. She won't leave them while she can ensure their safety."

"But by staying, she risks that!" Abrahm barks. "If she stays with them and then is discovered as a Lycan, they will all be in danger because they will think that they are all Lycans. They will all be interrogated and poked and prodded. There is nothing they won't do to suss out intruders if one is found."

"Not to interrupt your important discussion," Zoya inserts before Themis can respond. "But I hear Cleo coming. She'll be walking through the trees any moment."

Both Themis and Abrahm turn to where Zoya gestures just as Cleo pushes aside the branches. Zoya notices the determined, slightly dangerous glint in her eyes and the flash of her red hair as she tucks a stray lock behind her ear.

Here we go. Zoya backs away and stays further from the Alpha radiating power and determination. *I'm going to keep out of this fight.* She knows that Cleo is stubborn, but she also knows that Abrahm is determined to keep his daughter safe no matter what happens. "I'm going into the human settlement with my friends tomorrow." The bold and matter-of-fact tone

Cleo uses is no surprise to Zoya. "I will not leave them alone. If I do, they will know something is up."

"You're not going into that Lycan death trap and that is final!" Abrahm snarls, moving forward with his shoulders hunched as if expecting a fight. "I will not watch my daughter fall into the hands of those human monsters!"

"I don't care!" Cleo barks back at him and Zoya can almost see her hackles rise. "If I don't go with my friends, they are going to start searching for me. I've come this far with them. I will go into that settlement with my friends and I will live like a human. No one will discover what I am. I will be able to live like my friends and be able to get through this chapter of my life without any big problems."

"Cleo, see sense." Themis holds up a hand to Abrahm and starts with a cajoling tone instead of a demanding one. "If you go with your friends, you will have to hide who you are forever. You will have to sustain yourself on scraps of raw meat and eat them in your human form whenever you are one hundred percent alone. You can never have a true life there because any children you have will almost certainly be either Lycans or latent Lycans. You will have to be extremely careful."

"But—" Cleo tries to interrupt but Themis holds up his hand.

"You might be able to keep yourself hidden for a time, but people will always be suspicious of you." Themis looks at her meaningfully. "You won't be able to eat the food you are given. You will constantly be disappearing to eat the raw scraps you can scavenge. It will be just like it was on your journey here. You will suppress your new nature so much that it will start to lash out in uncontrollable and unforeseeable circumstances and someone will eventually discover what you are. If you aren't killed on sight, you'll be imprisoned and tortured for information about Lycans. Your friends will be kidnapped and tortured to determine if they are Lycans themselves. You will die knowing that your friends faced the same torture and death that you did before them."

"I have been able to pass as a human for almost two months." Cleo finally takes the opportunity to speak when Themis pauses for breath. "I have an idea of how I can keep myself under the human radar." She turns to Abrahm. "When you met my mother and were with her in that settlement, how did you pass for human? I'm sure you had to eat meals with them when they ate. I'm sure they were suspicious of you when you first showed up."

"I ate when I had to," Abrahm admitted, shrugging out of his half crouch. "I didn't enjoy the food, but I was able to stomach it for a while."

"I will be able to do the same." Cleo's voice is certain. "I've already tested the theory. We have venison jerky that Elijah makes at night. I've been able to stomach several strips of it as we've walked today. I think part of it is because I've finally been able to eat raw meat. If I can get my meat myself, I can ensure that I eat enough raw meat to survive eating the cooked meat I am given at mealtimes."

"But when would you eat the raw meat?" Abrahm asks, his voice a bit calmer than it was when she had first appeared. "You can't just go around eating raw meat in the middle of the settlement."

"I plan on offering my services as a hunter," Cleo says without hesitation. "I will hunt for the food. I'll be able to catch more food than the humans, even if I'm eating every other rabbit I find. I've been practicing using my hearing to find prey while we walked today. I can hear a chipmunk fart nearly a mile away. I can hear you guys blundering around about two miles out. I shouldn't have a lot of trouble finding food."

"But what if you have to go out with a partner or a group?" Themis demands. "I'm sure they'll notice if you start disappearing on them and coming back laden with animal carcasses."

"I'll make do," Cleo says to cover her uncertainty. "I won't be with a partner all the time. I'll be able to hunt for myself and I'll be able to get the food that I need. And if anything, I could probably ask for raw meat to cook myself. That shouldn't be too difficult."

As everyone seems to have calmed down, Zoya steps forward to speak for the first time. "What if we hang around here for a week?" she asks Abrahm. "Cleo can go into the settlement with her friends, but we'll hang around here for a week. After a week, you can decide whether to stay, and you can come out as if hunting and meet with us here. That way you can let us know how your plan is working. We will stay here, only moving if forced to do so by hunting parties. If you don't come to us after a week, we will wait three more days before making plans to come into the settlement after you. If you don't come out after that week and three days, we will assume that someone recognized you as a Lycan and we will rescue you." Zoya pauses. "Does everyone think that this is a good compromise for us to work with now?" She looks at the three other faces.

Cleo ponders the idea for a moment before nodding thoughtfully. Themis glances at both Abrahm and Cleo, furrows his brow and then nods at Zoya. Only Abrahm takes more than a minute to decide.

Abrahm paces before Zoya, going over her plan in his head several times. He huffs, pauses, turns to face everyone, then turns and continues to pace. Finally, after about five long minutes of this behavior, he finally faces all of them and nods.

"Fine," he says. "But I will only wait for one week. If you don't come out by that time, we will all be coming in the next day. We will find you and fight our way out with you. They won't get you." He looks at Cleo with a soft, fatherly expression.

"I won't let them," she returns to him, her determined expression matching his. Zoya smiles and turns away. "Now I need to eat and catch a dog or something before I head back to camp. Do you guys have any suggestions? I told my friends that I was using the meat for snares." Zoya peeks over her shoulder to see Cleo holding Themis's old satchel open, displaying several small chunks of raw meat inside.

"I'll get a few for you," Zoya offers. "I wanted to get some hunting done before the storm gets really bad. I'll be back in about an hour." And with that, she disappears into the woods with a wave of Cleo's gratitude.

*   *   *

The big day had arrived. Elijah sighs as he stretches and rolls over in his sleeping bag, feeling and hearing the squish of water outside the tent on the ground. He winces and sits up, looking around the cramped tent. Charlie lies in the sleeping bag next to him, still snoring softly and shivering slightly. Elijah shivers a little bit both in sympathy as well as with an actual chill that hangs in the air.

It's chillier this morning, he ponders, pulling his pack toward him for fresh clothes. *I hope it doesn't snow at all.* He pulls his clothes on quickly and then yanks on an extra sweatshirt. He rolls his sleeping bag up and attaches it to his pack before ducking out of the tent. Outside, Cleo paces in front of the entrance to where their tents are sheltered beneath the overpass. She glances over at him momentarily, then goes back to her pacing without comment.

"Good morning," Elijah says, putting his bag down on a raised chunk of cement. Cleo nods but doesn't respond. "How did you sleep?"

"Fine." Cleo's responses are short and clipped. "You?"

"Not bad," Elijah responds, moving to prod the fire. "It's colder now. I'm hoping the bad weather clears up. I don't like the idea of walking into the Northern Settlement soaking wet and bedraggled." He cracks a smile to get Cleo to warm up with him but it doesn't work. She seems distracted and hardly to have heard his joke.

Cleo nods distractedly and continues to pace, her steps getting faster and harsher as she moves. Elijah closes his eyes, takes a deep breath, and moves forward. He catches Cleo's left hand and pulls her out of the ditch she was starting to wear into the dirt beneath her feet. Startled, she attempts to yank her hand away, but Elijah keeps her hand in a tight grip and moves her so that they are face to face.

"Cleo, if you keep pacing, you're going to make yourself and me dizzy," he says, catching hold of her chin and keeping her attention. "What's going on with you? Are you nervous? We all are. We're hoping to be taken in by complete strangers in this new settlement. We have no idea what to expect other than other humans. I'm sure we'll be able to make a new home here. But we'll only know once we get through those walls." He smiles at her.

"I know." She grins sheepishly at him and lowers her eyes. "I'm just so unsure about what is going on. I don't know. I just want to be able to get us to a safe place."

"We've just been traveling for too long." Elijah leans forward and kisses Cleo briefly on the lips. He feels her stiffen and pulls away looking at her. "What? We've done that before. Charlie and Mandi are both still asleep. What are you worried about?"

Cleo closes her eyes and turns her head. "I'm just too high strung. I can't think about that right now. I'm too worried and stressed about things." Cleo pulls out of Elijah's now slack grip. "I'm sorry. I just can't think about anything but getting us this last little way to safety." And without a backward glance, she disappears into the still dripping trees.

About two hours later, with the sun starting to peek through the trees above the horizon to the east, their camp is packed up and the fire out. Charlie leads the way this time, following the overgrown highway toward the settlement. Elijah and Mandi follow on either side of him with Cleo pulling up the rear behind them all.

It takes almost four hours for them to be in full view of the wall when they hear the shouts of the guards. They are ordered to stop where they are and about two dozen men and women rush from the opening gates of the wall.

"Who are you?" the leader demands as he gets within ten yards of them. "State your names and your purpose! Now!"

Cleo pushes her way forward in front of the group. "My name is Cleota Estelle. My friends and I are from the Nashville Settlement. Our settlement was attacked and several of our friends and relatives were killed about two months ago. We left for the chance to find a safer home. We hoped we would find that at this settlement."

The soldiers approach slowly, their weapons drawn. Cleo and the rest of their group drop their weapons and keep their hands raised to look as harmless as possible. Cleo and her friends are completely disarmed and escorted by three people each. The leading soldier and three of his helpers carry the band's packs and escort the four newcomers through the gates.

Once inside the walls, Cleo, Elijah, Mandi, and Charlie are each escorted to separate rooms with two interrogators. Elijah's interrogators are a man in his thirties or forties and a young woman in her twenties. They ask questions about where they are from, where they had stopped, the route they had taken. They question him about his traveling companions and about the companion they lost.

The questioning goes on for what seemed like hours. When they finally allow Elijah to leave the interrogation room, he walks into their waiting room area to find Charlie and Mandi but no Cleo.

"What's going on?" he asks his friends. "Where's Cleo? How long have you guys been out here?" Charlie keeps glancing around as if expecting to see Cleo coming out of any of the doors around them. Mandi just sits, staring blankly at the wall in front of them.

"I've been here only a few minutes," Charlie says, continuing to fidget and look around. "Mandi was here before I was but not by much. Cleo's in one of the other interrogation rooms. I think they're questioning her more thoroughly than we were because she got injured and they want to be sure she isn't contaminated. They poked and prodded at me for a while to make sure I wasn't a Lycan or anything. I'm assuming they did the same thing with you?" Elijah nods at his question. "I'm just hoping Cleo comes out soon. I'd like to get started settling into this new spot."

"Me too," Mandi pipes up, finally glancing up at Elijah and Charlie. "I want to get a room in a building that I can have to myself. I'm going to decorate it and make it my own and no one can get me to move out or go back out to the wilderness ever again."

Elijah rolls his eyes at Mandi's daydreaming and her lack of compassion about their leader being kept under interrogation far longer than any of them. Elijah hadn't brought Mandi's betrayal up to any of their friends and hadn't talked about it during the interrogation, but he wonders if that might have been a mistake. If Cleo had known, maybe she would have treated Mandi a lot differently.

As Cleo is kept in the interrogation for another hour and the more time passes, the more both Elijah and Charlie grow restless and agitated. By the time she walks out of the room furthest from where they uncomfortably sit, both Elijah and Charlie cry out in excitement.

"What was taking so long?" Elijah demands, glaring at the two soldiers that stand as book ends on either side of Cleo.

"They just wanted to be one hundred percent sure that I'm not a Lycan." She sighs, shrugging uncomfortably and rubbing her injured arm. "They were pretty thorough."

"So, what now?" Mandi demands, ignoring Cleo's words and looking at the soldiers expectantly. "Do we get to see where we're living now? I want to go to sleep. It's been a long month of walking every day."

In fact, the soldiers do lead them to a nearby building where they are instructed to enter a set of two adjacent rooms. The boys take one room, the girls take the other, only to find two rows of about six bunkbeds on either side of the door. Mandi's grumblings of protest are shushed and scolded by Cleo as they unpack and Elijah grins at the indignity Mandi must deal with.

"I'm not sure what Mandi expected," Charlie mutters, unpacking his clothes and supplies from his bag and laying them on the top bunk over where Elijah unpacks his own possessions. "We haven't been here longer than a few hours. We haven't brought anything, and we don't have any money to speak of. It's not like we were going to just be handed a house to ourselves. We need to find out where we will fit in."

Elijah nods in agreement and hears Cleo explaining the same information to Mandi next door over the mild hum of activity in the rest of the building.

Once they are unpacked, another group of people in uniform, different from those uniforms of the soldiers that have brought them there but still a uniform of some importance, comes to lead them around the area where they will be living. Cleo is excitedly talking to these strangers, mentioning she'd like to join a hunting party. Elijah grins at the thought of Cleo's prowess with her bow and arrow and thinks that if these people didn't put a bow in her hands soon they are crazy.

It takes the rest of the day to learn about what they will be expected to do and where they will be expected to be the next day. Those in charge have agreed to allow Cleo to prove her skills at hunting the next morning, so she sits happily at the cafeteria table they have sat at for dinner. It is strange to Elijah to sit in a cafeteria after a month of finding and cooking their own food. The stew in front of him is delicious but far richer than he and the others are used to. He can only stomach a few bites of the savory chunks of meat that is well-seasoned. The pepper burns his tongue, as do the other spices in the dish. He sighs at the thought of finally being able to eat more than just bland food anymore.

Everyone heads to bed quickly after dinner, their stomachs full and satisfied for the first time since they had left the Nashville Settlement. Elijah hears Mandi and Cleo bickering slightly as well as meeting some of the other girls in their shared room before going in to meet the others that he and Charlie haven't met yet.

The next few days go by swiftly. Cleo becomes one of the hunters that go out daily. Mandi is brought to join some of the other ladies of the settlement in producing clothing and other necessary cloth and fabric materials. Charlie joins a group of farmers, eager to help with the raising of the local herds of sheep and goats as well as other food stuffs planted in the surrounding fields. Elijah visits several job centers, trying to find a good place for his handyman abilities. He settles on working with a blacksmith who works primarily on weaponry and other tools used in the settlement. Elijah begins his apprenticeship after the third day, and when he gets to the cafeteria at the end of the first day, he is exhausted.

Cleo sits down across from him, smiling at his drooping head and slow, almost weak movements as he tries to feed himself. "Busy day? Or have you just finally hit your exhaustion limit?" Her tone is teasing and light, but he can sense there is something beneath her teasing.

"The blacksmith just decided to give me some of the heaviest metals and things to carry around the shop," Elijah responds. "What about you? Find any more dogs or anything while you were out today?"

"Got some good meat today," she says, pushing the meat and potatoes around her plate. "I get to keep a portion of everything I catch and bring back to the settlement." She grins, but he can sense her hesitation. He also notices that, despite her having been sitting for almost ten minutes, she hasn't eaten much of her food. Maybe a bite or two but nothing more than that.

Their conversation devolves into eating and playing with the food before Cleo stands up abruptly. Elijah moves to follow her lead, but she waves him to sit down. "I'm just not feeling great. I'm going to turn in early. I'll talk to you tomorrow," she says, moving toward the exit.

Elijah sits again, but when she exits the cafeteria room, he stands and follows her at a distance. He follows her outside, a suspicious move as she said she wanted to turn in early. She moves across the road in front of the building where they were living and ducks into a shadowed alley. She continues to follow the alley and cuts into what seems like an abandoned and crumbling down building. By the time he follows her into the building, she's disappeared again, but he hears rustlings and rumblings nearby. He turns and sees a crouching figure ripping at a large chunk of raw meat. The fur over its body is a rich auburn that shimmers in the dimmed light from outside the building, but Elijah is frozen by the fear of coming upon a Lycan within the walls of the settlement. He gasps in shock and the creature glances up, startled with a bloody face, its fangs bared.

And then it freezes at the sight of him and the expression changes from one of anger to one of shock and fear. Suddenly, the face begins to change and in less than a minute,

Cleo stands in front of him with blood running down her face, but her hands reaching for him.

"Eli," she starts, her voice rough but clear. "I need you to listen to me. I know what this looks like, but I need you to hear me out."

Shaking with fear from when he had first seen the Lycan body, Elijah blinks at the frame of his best friend, then takes a shaky breath. "Can you clean your face?" It is the first thing that comes to his lips. Cleo lets out a startled chuckle in reaction.

"Give me a few minutes, okay?" She grimaces as her tongue touches the blood on her lips. "I need to finish eating really quickly. I'm starving. Then I'll clean myself up." At Elijah's nod, she transforms again into the form of a Lycan. She turns around and finishes the last few mouthfuls of meat before licking her hands and face clean. When she turns back to him, her face is clean and human again.

"What happened?" Elijah asks, moving closer to her now that she is normal-looking again. "I mean, how long have you been like this?"

"Since the attack that killed Kiya," Cleo responds, blushing. "Well, maybe a few days after that, but I've been struggling with it for over a week or so while we were traveling."

Elijah blanches. "So, you're a Lycan? You turned into one of those monsters?" He sees her wince and immediately regrets his words. "I'm sorry. I didn't mean that. But how can you look human?"

"I'm not like the Lycans that attacked us," Cleo says in defense of herself. "There are different levels of Lycans. The ones that attacked us were Omegas. They're the lowest, most bloodthirsty and weakest of the lot. I'm an Alpha. I'm one of the most powerful Lycans around. Most of the Omegas can't transform at all. I can keep myself looking human. I learned how to control myself with the help of two other Alphas and a Beta that were watching out for us while we traveled north. They protected us and fought off most of the Omegas that tried to hurt us. If it weren't for them, we all would have been killed by the big pack of Omegas that killed Kiya. They just got overwhelmed. They taught me how to control my powers as well as how to eat so that I don't have to hurt anyone. I just need to keep eating raw meat."

"So, you're safe?" Elijah asks, taking her hands hesitantly. "You haven't hurt anyone? You've figured out how to be a human?"

Cleo nods. "I'm in control of myself, but I can't eat raw meat as a human," she says, the feeling of the blood of the meat she had just finished still on the back of her tongue. She swallows hard before continuing. "I have to find a secure place to hide when I eat. I found this place yesterday and was able to bring my food from the hunt today here to hide it until after dinner, but this was the first time I've been able to eat raw meat since we've arrived. I can't keep going for as long as that between meals. I was starting to get desperate when I slipped out after dinner. I couldn't have waited much longer."

"So, you need to keep eating raw meat to keep yourself safe?" Elijah asks. "Why can't you just ask to have your meat cooked a little less than everyone else's?"

"I don't want to risk having even more attention drawn on me," Cleo admits. "We're already under so much scrutiny as it is. Anyhow, and I might get arrested or imprisoned. I couldn't do that to you guys, and I certainly don't want to put myself through that. It's best that I just keep finding hidden spots to eat."

"I could help you," Elijah offers. "I could guard wherever you are eating. I could make a bunch of noises to alert you if anyone comes upon you. Or have you already figured out how you are going to continue to go about everything?"

"I think I have a plan," Cleo says confidently. "I have proven myself more than an adequate hunter, and I think my fellow hunters realize that I do my best hunting on my own. They've agreed to let me go out on my own tomorrow, as long as I check in with the team leader every couple of hours. So that will be good. I can eat a little bit while hunting, and then be set every day."

Elijah nods slowly, taking in Cleo's plan. "I think that could work, but how much raw meat do you need to eat per day or per week to stay safe? Would you be able to eat enough?" He surveys her critically. "I don't want you to get into trouble, but I also don't want you to hurt yourself while you are trying to stay out from under everyone's scrutiny."

"I will eat enough," Cleo reassures him, her smile soft. "But I appreciate your concern. Now we should head back. I'm sure you're exhausted and I'm rather tired myself. I also need to be up early to head out hunting. We'll talk more about this soon. I'll let you know if I need a guard over my extracurricular dining."

And with that, they leave one by one to find their beds and get some sleep.

*   *   *

We need to talk to Abrahm by tomorrow, Cleo reminds herself for the fourth time that day as she enters the compound weighed down by four rabbits, a few wild birds, and a pack of other smaller animals she had caught and killed during her second solo hunt. She grins proudly to herself. Her hunt leader was impressed with what she had brought down with only her bow and arrow. She knows her own skills but doesn't want to bring more than the typical attention. As she moves toward the skinning shed where her catch will be skinned and prepared for her, Charlie runs up to her, grabbing her by the shoulders.

"Have you seen Eli?" Charlie gasps, out of breath. "I've been searching everywhere for him. I can't find him. He told me to meet him for lunch but never showed. I looked at the blacksmith's where he was apprenticed, but the smith said that Elijah left for lunch and never came back. I haven't seen him anywhere else."

"Let me get this stuff to the skinning shed and I'll help you look." Cleo pulls her burden from her shoulders and darts as quickly as she can toward the shed and leaves instructions with the head butcher to keep a portion of the meat to the side for her.

Without another look back at the shed, Cleo hurries to the building they were all staying in to begin their search. Charlie, divining what Cleo would do based on previous experience, is standing outside his and Elijah's quarters. Cleo stops in front of him, noticing that Mandi is absent.

"Where's Mandi?" Cleo asks, almost immediately wishing she hadn't spoken. Charlie gives her a dirty look and rolls his eyes.

"She says she couldn't care less about where Elijah is," Charlie snarls. "She didn't even look up from her sewing when I burst into where she was. She just scoffed and went back to her work without a care in the world. I wasn't about to drag her kicking and screaming from her nice, cushy job."

Cleo laughs darkly before turning into the currently empty dorm room Elijah and Charlie share with the other newly arrived or poorer men.

"So, you guys planned to meet up for lunch before you both left for work in the morning?" she asks, looking at where their bunk is situated. She looks over the top bunk to see Elijah's blanket and pillow, freshly wrapped in a new pillowcase, nicely tucked in, and settled on the bed. His other stuff that they had carried with them is on the side of the bunk bed or on the small tray up near where his head would lay. "Did he seem strange when you guys parted ways? Did he say anything out of the ordinary? Did he seem excited or depressed?"

Charlie shakes his head. "He just reminded me that we were supposed to meet for lunch. We had planned to meet up last night, he was just reminding me so I would remember." Charlie frowns as he thinks back. "He seemed perfectly normal. Didn't seem out of sorts at all. He was just ready to go about the day without any problems."

"Well, I'm going to go talk to some of my hunting friends," Cleo says. "I want to see if I can talk to one of the soldiers that brought us into the city. I want to see if they've seen anyone or if they have been interrogating Eli again." She follows Charlie out of the room and heads back to the skinning shed, knowing that some of her friends will likely be looking to get their shares of the meat she had hunted that day.

The three men working in the skinning shed greet her and the third one passes her the portion of her meat that she has caught, waving away her thanks with a "think nothing of it" air that she appreciates all the more. Two of the other men in the shed are from her hunting party earlier in the day and she approaches them openly, her package of meat safely tucked under her arm.

"If it isn't the queen of the wood," the first one says grandly, sketching a mock bow in her direction with a grin. His blue eyes are playful as he straightens himself and brushes the straw-colored hair back from his face. "What can we do for the best hunter in the settlement?"

"I need your help," Cleo says, smiling at their jokes. "I need to talk to one of the soldiers. One of my friends has gone missing and I was wondering if the soldiers had any idea of where he was. My brother was supposed to have lunch with him, and he never showed. We asked the blacksmith he was apprenticing with and he said that Elijah had left for lunch and never came back. Do you guys have any ideas of who I could talk to?"

The two hunters frown at each other, both thinking. The blond one scratches his chin, but his partner speaks first. "My brother works for the soldiers. I could ask him to bring one of the soldiers out here after dinner."

"That would be great, Henry." Cleo smiles at him. "Should I meet you back here to meet with them?"

"I'll bring them both out here in about two hours," Henry replies. "Does that work with you?" Cleo nods and they part ways. Ducking into the darkened alley, she makes her way through the busy streets. Her stomach growls as she passes stalls of cooking meat and other scents as she finds a little secret place to eat. She finds another ruin of a building and ducks through one of its doors.

Once inside, Cleo finds herself a quiet space in the center of the building to settle into her small feast. She rolls her head on her shoulders in her triggering movement and becomes her Lycan self before devouring the chunks of meat she received from the skinning shed. It takes her only a few minutes to eat, but as she finishes, she hears rustlings near the building and freezes. A full minute goes by and nothing happens. Cleo hesitantly turns back to her meal, only about three mouthfuls of meat remain as well as a bit of clean up left to do before she can head to the dorm to eat a more human dinner. But the rustling happens again, this time within the walls where she crouches over her meal.

Without warning, Elijah bursts through one of the doorways into where Cleo eats, his eyes wide with terror.

"Run!" he yells at her, and without a second's hesitation, she takes his advice and bolts.

Still in her Lycan form, Cleo can sprint out of the building and into the main streets of the settlement in seconds. She barrels through the dwindling crowds of people who leap aside with screams of terror or shouts of revulsion. Without thinking about where she is going, Cleo takes the shortest distance between where she is and the exit gate of the settlement. Knowing there will be soldiers, she tries desperately to keep herself moving in an erratic direction to get through and into the woods without getting shot.

As she approaches the gate, the shouts of soldiers raise in alarm go up and she finds her way blocked by heavily armed men and women. She darts between most, quicker and more agile than their human forms can keep up with. It is only when she reaches the gap between the gate that her path becomes more congested and she needs to slip between legs and under reaching arms.

The walls of the settlement fall behind her at last and she glances back to gauge her chances of making it to the woods when she hears the first of five shots ring out. She feels the sharp burn of at least one contacting her flesh and suddenly the world goes black.

CHAPTER TEN

Well, they're all a buzz. Themis watches through the trees close to the edge of the settlement, sniffing after a few foxes and wild dogs that had skulked through the area recently. *It looks like the place is an ant hill that some idiot kid kicked around.*

Shouts and screams reach him on the breeze, and he focuses in on the large open gates. Without realizing what he is seeing, Themis focuses in the center of the open gates where a lone figure races across the barren expanse. Upon closer inspection, he realizes that the racing figure isn't human but Lycan. Another second and Cleo's distorted features stand out distinctly, causing Themis to cry out in alarm.

Several armed men run after Cleo, their faces grimaces of disgust and fear. One or two fire off shots at their quarry and Cleo stumbles into the dirt.

Restraining himself against an almost unbearable urge to run out after her, Themis growls to himself and watches closely to ensure he sees her chest rise and fall. He hadn't seen any spurts of blood, but he wanted to make sure. He focuses on Cleo's chest and spots the tell-tale rise and fall of her chest.

With that certainty, Themis bolts back into the woods. It takes him only five minutes to sprint back to where Abrahm and Zoya had set up camp. When he blunders into the clearing, he is gasping for breath.

"Cleo... soldiers...." He struggles to push the words out. "Guns... breathing!"

Zoya looks at her Alpha, blinking slowly as if trying to read his mind. "Themis, breathe. Deep breath in, then out. In, then tell us what's going on." Themis rolls his eyes but does as she suggests.

"Cleo's been captured," he states baldly when he gets enough air in his lungs. Abrahm immediately jumps to his feet.

"Where?" he demands. "What happened?" The intensity of his gaze as he grabs Themis's forearm shocks the other Alpha.

"She bolted out of the settlement fully transformed." Themis puts a hand up to still the older Lycan. "Some soldiers shot her, and she fell." Abrahm gasps but Themis talks over any protests. "She's breathing. I made sure of it before I left the edge of the woods."

"They know what she is." Zoya's tone is dark, malicious. "If they didn't kill her as she ran away, they must think they can use her for something."

Abrahm gives her a dark look. "They'll try to get her to tell them how she managed to pass as a human." His voice drops to a growl. "They'll torture her and there's nothing I can do about it! This is exactly why I didn't want her going in there in the first place!" He lashes out at a nearby tree, transforming and slashing the thick trunk with his claws.

"We need a plan." Zoya watches Abrahm's display of agitation calmly, her mind already thinking of ways they might get to Cleo. "Themis, didn't you say you had met up with Cleo's brother in the woods with Cleo a few days ago?"

Themis nods, his mind still trying to cope with the realization that Cleo was in danger. "Yeah. He didn't seem too pleased with me, though."

"Never mind that now," Zoya plows through his words. "Would you be able to recognize him again if you saw him?"

"I think so." Themis thinks back with difficulty. He recalled the young man who had come looking for Cleo when she was struggling with her identity.

"All you guys need to do is get into the settlement and find the brother." Zoya's words light a tiny spark of hope in Themis's chest.

"Are you feeling more confident about your transformations?" Abrahm asks, looking at Themis with concern. "Do you think you could keep it up for a few days?"

"I think so." Themis looks at Zoya. "Charlie didn't notice anything amiss when he found me with Cleo. I think I could keep the transformation if I needed to."

Zoya begins to pace, speaking aloud to make sure the two Alphas understand what she is thinking. "You guys need a cover story to get in," she begins. "If I remember correctly, you told Charlie that you were part of the small settlement that helped Cleo, right?"

"I told him that," Themis agrees, watching Zoya pace. "I don't think I told him much more than that though, and I don't think we even told him where exactly the settlement was."

"That's not a big deal," Abrahm breaks in. "Most of the small settlements like to keep their locations secret to prevent packs of Lycans from finding them and taking them over."

"Perfect," Zoya continues her thoughts. "So, you two can explain that you're just coming to check on a group of travelers that had passed through your land recently. Describe the four of them, ask if they've seen any of the humans around."

"We'll need to be pretty specific about the details of the settlement," Abrahm warns, glancing now at Themis. "Our stories need to match. They'll interview us separately and check to see if the stories line up. Usually they'll interview one first and then the other."

"But Cleo's stuck in there now!" Themis snarls, his adrenaline suddenly surging again. "We need to get her out!"

"It will take them a few days before they start really torturing her." Abrahm settles a hand on Themis's shoulder. "We have a little time. Let's use it to best effect and make sure our plan is pretty darn fool proof. That way, we know we'll get Cleo out."

And with that, the three Lycans set to work.

*   *   *

We're finally safe! Mandi grins to herself as she spins yarn in the main workroom with several other women. She nudges her neighbor playfully as they continue their work.

"How are you feeling today, Mandi?" An elderly woman several places down the wall glances up briefly from her finished ball of yarn. "You were a bit flustered yesterday evening."

"Oh, I'm feeling much better this morning." This is true, as far as anyone else is concerned. She knows she should feel honored to be among this prestigious group of women, but she just cannot get over the knowledge of just how inferior she is compared to them. Sitting in this room reminds her just how insignificant she truly is in this settlement. "I think everything has settled down for the most part." She smiles at her companions and continues with her work.

"That's good, my dear." The woman on Mandi's right lays a quick hand on her shoulder in support. "I hope everything continues to work well for you. I heard there was a nasty bit of business earlier today about some Lycan getting into the settlement in disguise! I thought we were all supposed to be safe here! Now we come to find out that these monsters can come and live among us, hidden and waiting to strike." The older woman shudders somewhat theatrically. "Thank God the soldiers got her before she could wreak havoc on us all."

"Too true!" one of the other older ladies echoes parrot-like. Mandi grins. All these women felt like home. She remembers the older ladies at her old settlement had taken her under their wing before. Now these lovely women and girls were taking care of her. It felt good, almost as if she is finally in a home.

"Mandi!" Charlie's slightly panicked shout breaks the calm, homely silence of wool working and the weaver's trade. "Mandi! Where are you!?" And suddenly he bursts through the door to the weaving room Mandi sits in. He spots her almost instantly and hurries toward her. She doesn't move, keeping her eyes on her work.

"What do you want, Charlie?" she demands in a flat tone. "As you can see, I'm quite busy and don't have time to deal with whatever problems you're trying to bring to me to fix."

"I need your help." Charlie stands in front of her, almost bouncing on the balls of his feet. "Elijah went missing yesterday, and now Cleo's gone! I need your help to try and find them! They've got to be around here somewhere!"

"Well, I don't know about you..." Mandi begins with a sigh, glancing up at the ceiling above her as if searching for patience. "But I thought that Cleo seemed to be up to something. I told the soldiers when we got here that she had started to act weird on our way here. Wherever Cleo and Elijah are, I'm sure they're where they need to be."

It's not as though they didn't ask for it, she thinks privately to herself. *Cleo was disappearing for hours at a time the last few weeks. Even after she was gone for a few days after she got hurt. She needed to be watched. She could have been bitten and we might not have known.*

In front of her, Charlie is gesticulating, saying something about their friends. Mandi waves away his babbling with a flick of her wrist before returning to her spinning.

"I'm sure the soldiers found whatever Cleo has been doing rather interesting, and I'm sure Elijah is being interrogated about Cleo's activities. She's been all over the place." Mandi sighs. "Now if you don't mind, I need to get back to work." She barely finishes her sentence before Charlie's hand catches her a stinging slap across the face.

"You cow!" Charlie yells. "Your friends are likely locked up somewhere and you don't care?"

"Who the hell do you think you are, Charlie Estelle?" Mandi demands, coming out of the shock of the slap almost immediately and standing up. "You come in here, demand my help, then slap me? Go screw yourself! I hope you join Cleo and Eli, wherever they are. You all deserve each other!"

"You're our friend, Mandi!" Charlie shouts back at her. "Or I thought you were! What about Kiya? Did her death mean nothing to you?"

"It did," Mandi says baldly. "I watched her die and would do it a hundred times over again! She was a burden on all of us! We had to take turns guarding with her because she couldn't see out of her one eye! We gave up hours of sleep just to babysit her. I was relieved when she—!"

Before she knows exactly what is happening, Charlie's hands are wrapped around her throat, shaking her violently. She sputters and swats weakly at his arms as he bellows and pulls her from her seat, knocking over the spinning wheel and pushing her up against a wall. Her hands beat frantically against his face and hands.

Then suddenly, she is sprawled on the floor, gasping for air, lying on the floor in front of the wall. Three or four ladies crowd around her, their twittering voices unable to quite break through the fog left by Charlie's hands.

"I was right to tell the soldiers," she gasps, watching dazedly as Charlie is dragged away by a couple of soldiers who had burst in at the racket. "You're all crazy!" She slowly sits up, leaning heavily against the support of the women circling her like buzzards.

Together, three of them manage to walk her slowly to the dormitories used by the sewing and weaving ladies who do not have a house with a husband or family. They tuck her up gently in bed and ply her with tea and other beverages to try and help her throat heal as well as keep her calm.

"Don't you worry about that boy," one of the younger girls says. "I'm sure they'll sort him out. You just keep yourself in bed. We'll keep an eye on you for the next few days."

And they are true to their word. Not an hour goes by when someone doesn't peek in to check if she needs anything. Mandi smiles to herself, feeling properly warm and well taken care of for the first time in weeks, if not months.

It's not like any one of my so-called friends did anything to keep an eye on me, she muses to herself. *All they cared about was getting to the new settlement and following Cleo into whatever traps were lying in wait. Now I'm finally being treated the way someone ought to be treated.* And with that comforting thought, she curls up to take a nice nap before diner.

*   *   *

A sharp ache in the center of her back brings Cleo to consciousness roughly in fits and starts. She grimaces and clenches her eyes shut as if to defend against the intrusion of sensation and awareness.

Just like Mandi to wake me up by jamming a rock right underneath my back instead of just shaking me like a normal person, she thinks to herself as she rolls on to her side to try and escape the pain. When shifting positions doesn't provide any relief, she sighs.

"Alright." She pushes herself from her side into a seated position without opening her eyes, half noticing that the ground beneath her hands is smooth instead of the rough, pine-strewn floors she had grown accustomed to on their journey. She scrubs at her face and stretches, jerking to a stop as her movements trigger sharper pain in her back. Her eyes fly open in shock.

What is this? she asks herself as she stares dumbfounded at the stone walls around her. A bare globe of light glares down at her, bathing her surroundings in an ominous orange light. Across the room, a heavy metal door stands with a barred window covered on the outside by more metal. Looking closer, she sees a slot that seems to slide to the side but is currently closed.

Cleo glances down to find herself barely covered by the shredded rags of the clothes she had been wearing. The sight of her clothes brings back memories from before: Elijah bursting in on her eating, her mad dash from the abandoned building and transforming into her Alpha state. Then the sharp prick of multiple projectiles hitting her frame.

They have me! She stands and flings herself toward the door. She gets within three feet of it before something catches her around the torso and yanks her off her feet. The clink of chains makes her turn as she stumbles backwards. A length of the metal links attaches to the back wall by a well-bolted fixture. Cleo pushes the rags on her torso away to expose straps of leather crossing her chest going from above each shoulder down to just above the opposite hip. The straps are tight against her skin, thick as three of her fingers, and as she reaches over her shoulder, she realizes the pain in her back is likely coming from where the straps are connected to the chain.

the chain.

"Let me out!" she screams at the door. "Let me go!"

They're going to starve you, a small voice from the back of her mind breaks through into the forefront. *They're going to leave you in here forever and you'll never see Charlie, or Eli, or Themis, or Abrahm again! We're doomed! We're going to starve to death!*

Shut up! Cleo must bite her tongue to keep herself from screaming at the voice in her head. *They want information from me. They won't let me starve completely. I'm sure we've survived worse while walking with Charlie, Eli, and Mandi on our way here. We'll make it through this and I'm sure that Themis and Abrahm are already thinking of a way to get me out. I never checked in with them when I said I would, so they will be worried out of their mind for me.*

Maybe that's what the humans want, another, nastier voice breaks into her confidence. *Maybe the humans want to use you as bait to lure more Alphas in so that they can start to kill all the Lycans off, one by one.*

Cleo rolls her eyes. *That would be inefficient and stupid to use one Alpha to try and lure an entire species to their deaths.*

She shakes her head in wonderment at the thoughts. Her head had never been this crowded before. Usually she simply played "devil's advocate" with herself to make sure she checked out all possible outcomes of a situation. This is something different. It is almost as though her human and Lycan sides had two distinct personalities.

I'll have to ask Abrahm if he knows anything about latent Lycans having weird thoughts, she says, making a mental note to herself before turning to focus on the chains again. She steps closer to where the fixture is and studies it. Four bolts lock a square plate of metal to the center of the cement block wall. The chain running from her back attaches at a solid-looking D-shaped loop of metal welded into the plate.

Cleo takes the chain in her hands close to the D-loop and gives a jerk to it, focusing on the plate. It doesn't move, so she takes a firmer grip on the slippery metal links and settles her feet. She clenches her jaw and wrenches with all her strength against the chain, hauling against the bolted plate. A small trickle of dust sneaks from beneath the lower right bolt but nothing else moves. After a few seconds, she releases the chain and relaxes her stance. She huffs in frustration and takes a few deep breaths.

You know what you'll need to do, the nastier of the two voices in her head sneers from its back corner. *You'll need to transform. It's the only way you'll be able to get yourself out.*

Cleo closes her eyes, taking a deep breath to keep herself calm. When she opens them again, she responds to the voice. *I don't want to transform if I can help it,* she snaps. *I don't know who's watching and I don't want to give them any more information than they already have.*

This seems to satisfy the voice for the moment, and she returns to her task. She focuses her attention on the lower right bolt, as this is where the biggest weakness appears to be. She kneels beneath the plate, getting a closer look at the slight gap between the concrete and metal plate. She presses the fingertips of her left hand against the head of the bolt, brushing them one way and then another. The work is slow, but with determination the bolt slides free.

Sighing in relief, Cleo settles herself onto the ground to rest after her unknown length of time focusing on the delicate task. Her fingers ache and she clenches and unclenches them to work the stiffness from the tendons. She picks up the bolt with her right hand and sets it back into its spot to appear like it hasn't been moved.

As she turns to consider her surroundings more, the door across the room from her opens and two soldiers march in. Cleo tries to hurry to her feet, but as she staggers with the unaccustomed weight of the chains attached to her back, the soldier on her left lashes out and catches her across the face with the staff he carries in his hand. The blow lands at the point of her cheek, and as she is still unbalanced from the ungainly way she is forced to rise, she falls to her hands and knees. The crack of the hardwood against the bones of her face stuns her and the guard on the right takes advantage of her momentary stillness to kick her in the ribs.

Cleo's arms collapse from beneath her and she gasps, unable to draw in breath.

Get up! The angry voice bursts to the front of her consciousness immediately. *Fight these bastards! Kill them and escape!* Cleo almost feels a physical pull at her to get up. Her heart pounds frantically in her chest.

No! The scared voice's feeling of panic is nearly overwhelming. *Stay here! Let them hit you and they'll go away!*

Both of you shut up! Cleo almost screams at herself as the right guard pulls her to her feet and shoves his face into hers.

"Who else is working with you?" he demands, his spittle splattering over her cheeks. Cleo flinches away from him and manages to get her arms up to shove him away. She staggers as her feet find hard floor and tumbles against the back wall.

The other guard catches her shoulder and turns her so he has her back pinned against the wall with his forearm across her shoulders.

"Who else knew what you are?" he growls, his own staff held across her abdomen, blocking her arms to her side. "Tell me!"

"No one!" she snarls back at him. "Let me go!"

Surprising her, he flings her to the ground and the pair leaves. Stunned and gasping, Cleo glances after them as they close and bolt the door behind her. Minutes pass and she manages to find her feet again, standing to be prepared if another attack comes. Her breathing returns to normal again, and she winces as she prods her face with her left hand. Her left cheek feels swollen and tingly and when she prods the point of her cheekbone, pain shoots across the left side of her face.

You're an idiot! the angry, alpha voice roars at her in fury. *Why the hell didn't you fight back? We could have killed those idiots and they wouldn't bother us again! You need to grow up and fight back!*

They attacked us when we weren't prepared. the passive, Omega voice snarls back. *We couldn't have fought back! They came at us unprovoked! We need to just curl up and they'll leave us alone!*

Cleo sighs, beginning to get frustrated with how crowded her brain has become. She lets the two voices snarl at each other, debating how she should approach what might come next. She walks forward to where the chain limits her and narrows her eyes at the door before her. The metal blocking the barred window had been drawn aside, but no one stands right in front of the door. Three shafts of more artificial light shine into her cell, but not even shadows appear to give her an idea of her surroundings.

She turns back and begins to pace. Unable to tell the time by the sun or the change in light around her, she turns to the needs of her body to determine time. Her stomach begins to grumble gently, reminding her that she didn't know the last time she had eaten any meat. She had hardly been able to swallow more than a few mouthfuls when Eli had barged in to warn her that the soldiers were on to her.

She sighs, knowing that it will likely be a long few days.

The guards come in three more times before the glowing orb above her is shut off. Each time, the men stay for a short amount of time, surprising her when she is sitting or lying down to rest and not letting her get her feet under her enough to resist. Each time, they ask different sets of questions. The second and fourth time, they demanded that she transform and kept taunting her when they could kick her without retribution from her Lycan self. Those two times, the Alpha voice, as Cleo had begun to call the angry voice, became agitated to the point where it almost got full control. It took every ounce of concentration to prevent the Alpha from getting loose and making them transform.

The other times, they simply asked about how much Eli knew or who else knew what she was. It was strange.

When the light turned off, Cleo thought that they would leave her alone, but the questioning continued. It was random, unpredictable. By the time the light turned on again, Cleo could barely stand for exhaustion. She stayed on her feet until the next round of guards came in, but the pattern had changed.

This time, three men walked through the door instead of two. The two guards stood beside the door, but the third man walked forward, his hands raised.

"Who are you?" Cleo demands, settling herself into a defensive stance, prepared for a trick. "What do you want? I've told you all I know. There's nothing I can do for you."

The man's eyes rove over her with concern. "I'm not here to ask you anything. I was instructed to come here because one of our guards said you were being mistreated." His voice is soothing. "My name is Colonel Griffin. I'm in charge of this quarter of the settlement." He puts out a hand to her.

"Colonel?" Cleo asks, hesitating. "What's that?" She doesn't reach for the hand but stares at it in a half distrustful, half exhausted stare.

"Colonel means I am in charge." The man smiles lightly. "All of the soldiers and guards in this quarter answer to me and I answer to the commander of the Army who commands the entire settlement." The colonel motions for her to sit as he notices her shaking legs. "Please, sit. I'm not here to hurt you. I'm here to ensure you get the proper care while under my charge."

Not wanting to trust this stranger but realizing that she is going to fall if she doesn't sit soon, Cleo sits against the back wall. Her eyes lock on the two guards beside the door.

"They've come in here and beaten me," she growls, nodding at them and then brushing her hand against her swollen and painful cheek.

"Leave us!" Griffin orders, and to Cleo's surprise, both leave. As the door closes, he calls after them. "Send Private Gallagher with some food." A bark of "Yes, sir," and Griffin nods.

"What do you want?" Cleo demands again as the colonel sits in front of her. "I don't have anything else to tell you. They've tried to get me to talk, but I have nothing to tell them."

Griffin holds his hands out palm up in a placating gesture. "I don't want anything. I am here to determine if you need anything. It is my job to ensure anyone that is being held in our prisons is kept well and that nothing improper is going on. I will ensure that the two guards in charge of you are disciplined for their actions."

"They'd better be," Cleo snarls, barely loud enough for the colonel to hear. He tilts his head, regarding her curiously.

"Can you tell me what they did?" he asks. "Just so that I can have a record of it. My scribe is outside at the mirror and can hear and see what is going on. He is going to write down everything you say so that we have your testimony of what they did."

Cleo scrubs at her face, the fatigue of the last day catching up to her. She looks into Colonel Griffin's dark brown eyes and all of what had happened comes piling out of her in a rush. She explains in detail every hour that the thugs had been in her cell, Cleo yelling and shouting her frustration and anger. Griffin sits and listens, allowing her to say everything she wants to. When she finally stops speaking, her chest heaving from deep breaths to try and calm herself down, almost an hour has passed.

"Well," he begins, when there is a knock on the door, and he turns. "Ah, this must be Private Gallagher." He stands, leaving Cleo to recover on the floor. "I can only imagine you are famished." He opens the door, takes the tray from a young man barely older than Cleo who stands right outside the door. She doesn't get a good look at him from her place on the floor before the door shuts again. When the colonel turns to her, the smell of the hot cooked food on the tray hits her nose and her breath catches. She retches, curling up on herself and trying to get her stomach back under control, but the retching continues.

"Get it out of here!" she gasps, her stomach trying to empty itself, despite having nothing but bile left in it.

The colonel immediately opens the door again, orders the private outside to take it away and returns. A few moments pass and Cleo is finally able to regain control of herself enough to sit back against the wall to catch her breath.

"What happened?" Colonel Griffin asks, sitting down in front of her again, a look of concern on his face. "Was it the food? Did it not smell good? I didn't think chicken and rice had that strong of a smell."

"I can't eat cooked food," Cleo explains. "I'm sure you saw me when they captured me. I'm a Lycan. I can't eat your food." She pulls her knees up to her chest and hugs them, still feeling sick. "I prefer raw meat. I just can't digest cooked meat all that well, and the smell makes me sick."

"Well, I think I have all the information I need." The colonel stands and moves toward the door. "I will have a tray of meat brought so that you can eat and then you should get some sleep. We'll have another chat again soon."

Cleo nods and watches him leave before laying her head on her knees.

You shouldn't have talked to him, the Alpha voice rumbles at her, making her hackles rise a bit. *He can't be trusted! No one can be. You need to get out of here.*

Leave me alone! Cleo snaps at it, shaking her head. *I just need food and sleep. We'll figure out what to do when I've rested and gotten a little bit of strength back.*

And with that, she lies down and falls fast asleep.

*   *   *

This is intolerable, Themis thinks to himself, sitting in a hardbacked chair in a seven-by-nine-foot room. He stares at the window across the room from him where he can see three soldiers gesturing to another seated figure. The three green-clad figures move slightly and Abrahm is briefly visible talking with just as much animation as the men and woman around him. *I don't know how he sat in his room, watching me get interrogated.*

He recalls that his own questioning had taken almost three hours by the time they were satisfied with his answers and went next door to examine Abrahm. They had been thorough, to the point that Themis had experienced a moment of panic when he had forgotten how long it had been since Cleo was supposed to have joined with their pretend settlement. He had needed to take a moment to close his eyes to think. Almost as if Abrahm were whispering in his mind, he had recalled that they had agreed that they had come about a week prior to them arriving. He maintained the slight uncertainty that anyone would have if they just learned that someone in close contact with him had been found to be a Lycan.

We should have realized that security would be a hundred times tighter, Themis thinks to himself. *We must be the first people to come into the Settlement since Cleo and her friends. They were sure to have become super suspicious. It doesn't help that we are probably the last ones according to their records to see Cleo other than her friends before she apparently turned into a raging monster.*

Without warning, Abrahm's voice bursts into his head. *Will you shut up?*

Themis looks up, but Abrahm's face is hidden from view. Themis stands and begins to pace, needing something to do with himself instead of sitting and pondering their mistakes.

Surprisingly, Abrahm's interview takes only about an hour and before Themis knows it, Abrahm and a woman in the faded green of the military's uniform are standing in the doorway into Themis's interrogation room.

"If you'll follow me, Mr. Masters, I will show you and Mr. Rohnan to your quarters," the woman says, motioning for Themis to follow her. As she leads them into the corridor, she glances over her shoulder at them. "My name is Private Elsifer. If you need anything while you are staying here, don't hesitate to ask."

Abrahm nods and smiles politely at her, but Themis doesn't trust himself to do more than nod at her. Soldiers walk in front of and behind them, on errands for their commanders. Other stand in doorways, talking or joking with each other across the halls. None seem to give them much more than a cursory glance, but Themis feels as though they are all watching them like hawks. He glances sideways at Abrahm but doesn't catch his eye. Abrahm appears completely at his ease and easily smiles and nods at all the passing soldiers who nod back without looking twice at them.

When they finally reach the door onto the street, Themis gives a silent sigh of relief to be joining the bustling foot traffic. Along the streets they go, passing buildings in varying states of repair or disrepair. Several of the taller buildings appear to be uninhabited and the people seem to avoid the worst of the decrepit buildings for fear of collapse.

"Why are so many of the buildings falling down?" Abrahm asks, leaning forward for their guide to be able to hear his question.

"We don't have the supplies as of yet to tear down the worst of the buildings," she replies, glancing at a particularly sad five-story building collapsing in on itself. "Most people know by now which of the buildings are safe enough to go into, and we've done lots of repair work on all of the buildings that we can to make it possible for us to house so many. The council has made our quarter the next on the list for more repairs, but that could take time, as the North East quarter is the most heavily damaged now. We had some horrible storms this winter and several of the buildings that used to be structurally sound are now barely able to stay standing, let alone safe enough for people to enter them. For now, we just need to be patient."

She leads them north along the road that follows the path of the wall several hundred yards away on their left. Themis spots the guards walking two-by-two along the walkway at the top of the wall and sees at least six towers within their visual range. *This is going to be more dangerous than we thought,* he ponders to himself as they turn left and walk straight for a three-story building that appears well kept and sturdy.

"Welcome to the South-East Barracks," Private Elsifer states, opening the door for them. "We'll be going up to the second floor." She points toward a stone staircase to the right of the door. "Your room will be the first door on the left." They climb a flight of stairs, turn right and the first door on their left of the long hall stands open. Inside the room are two rows of six bunk beds lined up along the two walls. A window at the far end of the room shows the sky fading from a baby blue to pale gold with the sunset.

"Are any of the beds taken?" Abrahm asks, bringing Themis's attention to him. "Or should we just pick any of the beds?"

"I believe that the only beds not available are the two sets of bunks at the end." The private points. "You could take any of the others, if you'd like." She glances down the hall and then back at them. "Dinner is being served down on the first floor if you would like. Otherwise, I will leave you both to get settled in."

"Thank you for your assistance, Private," Abrahm replies, giving her a slight bow. "We will get settled and head down for dinner in a bit. I just have one more question, before you go." When the private looks up questioningly, he continues. "Will we have freedom to walk around the city as we wish, or do we need to be accompanied by a guard?"

"Oh..." The private's brow furrows. "I don't believe that my commander said anything about you needing guards. I will find out for you, but I think you both will be able to come and go around the settlement as you please. Just remember to follow any directions or orders given to you by soldiers. You are here as our guests, but you must follow our laws."

"Absolutely." Abrahm nods. "Please let us know what you find out from your commander. We will try to stay here for the rest of the evening if you hear anything that we need to know."

The private nods and walks back down the hall. Themis turns back to the room as Abrahm moves forward to the first bunk bed. He drops his bag on the bottom bed and looks at Themis.

"You don't mind sleeping on the top, do you?" he asks. Themis stares at him, dumbfounded. "The top bunk. I think it would be best if we stayed on the same bed. At least we know the other won't move much in their sleep," Abrahm clarifies, pointing to the mattress over where he had laid his own bag.

"How do you get up?" Themis asks, staring blankly at the bed. Abrahm sighs and demonstrates, putting his foot on the frame beneath the lower bunk near the head of the bed, then stepped up, pushing his hands on the upper mattress and curling his legs beneath him so that he was kneeling on the top bunk.

"It takes a bit of practice," Abrahm warns, settling himself to sit on the bed. "But I'm sure you'll manage. I just can't do it when I'm half awake. That and I know you don't move much when you sleep. I do, especially on soft beds, and it will be better if I'm closer to the ground in case I fall out of bed." And with that, he swings down gently, catching the foot hold of the lower bedframe before standing in front of Themis again.

Themis looks uncertainly at the metal framing as if not trusting it to take his weight, but he hoists himself up similarly to Abrahm and finds himself sitting starting at the doorway. "Not that hard," he says, catching sight of Abrahm's quickly stifled smirk. "I'll get better at it with a few tries."

Without another word, Abrahm settles himself on the bottom bunk and begins going through the two packs they brought with them. Most of the meat they had brought had been confiscated and given to the kitchens in this area of the settlement to help feed the rest of the people, but they each had been allowed to keep a large, almost three-pound steak a piece wrapped in oil skins to keep it fresh.

"We should save them," Themis says, attempting to climb down from his perch and succeeding awkwardly. "Who knows when we'll be able to get fresh meat again. We should try and put them in those personal cold boxes that are near the kitchens."

"If you're looking for somewhere to store those, I wouldn't leave them in here," a voice from the doorway recommends offhandedly. Themis glances up and starts in recognition. The other man stops dead as well, staring wide-eyed in shock as he gets a good look at Themis's face. "You!"

Themis stares blankly at Charlie, Cleo's brother. Abrahm straightens and glances between the two men as if watching a tennis rally. Finally, Themis finds his voice.

"Hello, Charlie," he says lamely. Charlie's face goes from white to a deep red in an instant and glares accusingly at Themis.

"What the hell are you doing here?" he snarls, pointing accusingly at Themis. "You were supposed to have stayed in the woods. You... you..." he sputters, as if unable to form a comprehensive thought.

"I'm here with a friend from my settlement," Themis interrupts the babbling. "This is Arthur. He's here to help. We came to make sure that you all made it to the settlement okay. When we arrived, we were told that you all arrived, but they refused to say where Cleo was. Have you heard anything?"

It takes Charlie a minute to allow his comprehension to overcome his astonishment. When he finally speaks, it is with a careful, almost overly controlled voice. "All I know is that I tried to find Eli and Cleo two days ago and couldn't. I went to find Mandi, and let my temper get the best of me." His blush betrays just how much his temper had betrayed him. "I just got out of the lock up after letting myself cool off. Thank God Mandi didn't push charges." The last seems to be more a thought to himself.

"Be that as it may, do you know what happened?" Themis breaks into Charlie's musings impatiently. "I heard that Cleo was discovered to be a Lycan. Do you know what they found out or how?"

Charlie shakes himself. "All I know is that a few days ago, Elijah disappeared. The next day Cleo was gone and word around the camp was that a Lycan had gotten into the settlement. The soldiers say they took it down, but that it's still alive somewhere in this quadrant, but no one knows any details."

Abrahm and Themis share a significant glance that Charlie doesn't miss. "What? You think that Cleo was the Lycan?"

"Charlie, we have reason to believe that your sister may have become a Lycan while on the road after she stopped at our settlement." Abrahm's voice is soothing. "The way the soldiers questioned us when we came in today, especially when they heard that we knew Cleo from her travels made me suspect that she is the one they are holding under suspicion of being a Lycan." Charlie's look of suspicion darkens at the words.

"If they think they can imprison her with no cause, then they have another thing coming," he vows, half turning toward the door. Themis catches him before he can get too far.

"There's nothing you can do," Themis says. "At least not now. We were concerned about all of you making it to the Northern Settlement, so we came looking for you. We're here to help, but I don't think we'll be able to reason our way past the guards to get her out. We think the only way that we'll be able to get Cleo out is to break her out of the prison."

Abrahm elbows Themis, reminding him to keep his voice down. Themis nods, lowering the volume of his voice. "The best thing you'll be able to do is get us as much information as you can about the area and where people might be held prisoner."

"I can do that," Charlie replies, nodding before he turns to the door. "I need to go to dinner. I will stop by tomorrow morning, or around lunchtime at the latest to check in with you." He turns to go, but then turns back. "The meat should go in the fridges down the hall. Make sure it's packaged in a way that you'll recognize, and you can grab it again later."

"Where are you staying?" Abrahm asks before he can walk away. "In case we find something urgent and we need to get a hold of you."

"I'm downstairs," he replies. "Just ask around for me and the boys will point you in the right direction. I'm with a bunch of other single men of the wall guard."

"Thank you, Charlie," Themis says, holding out his right hand. Charlie clasps it firmly before turning and heading out the door.

As Charlie walks down the hall, the men by the beds at the far end of the room stand and head toward the door. Themis and Abrahm stop speaking as the pair walks nearer to them, preferring to watch the strangers pass out into the hall and down the stairs toward the smell of cooking meat.

"What's the plan for tomorrow?" Themis asks after they are gone.

Abrahm shakes his head. "I've been thinking about that since we got out of the interrogation room. Once we hear back from the private about our restrictions around the settlement, I plan on taking advantage of the liberties we'll have to see the defenses of the settlement and to get an idea of potential escape routes."

"What do you want me to do?" Themis asks, his eyebrow cocked. "Stay here and wait for Charlie?"

"No." Abrahm shakes his head. "I want you to head further north, deeper into the settlement." He glances to the window. "See if you can spot any sign of a prison. Keep an ear out for any sound of Cleo too. Not that I'm expecting any overt sign of her, but we can't be too careful."

Themis nods and turns to face the bunk bed again. He sighs and attempts to climb up again.

*   *   *

Wake up! the voice in her head screams shrilly and Cleo sits bolt upright in a blind panic. Her eyes hardly register her surroundings as she moves from her side to her feet in seconds. She sways on her feet as her head spins and she struggles to maintain her balance. In the delayed surge of adrenaline following the shriek in her mind, Cleo realizes that there is nothing in the room with her; she is alone in the silence.

What the hell was that for?! she demands of the voices in her head. Neither one responds and she begins to pace to bring her heart rate back down. *There was no need to wake me up. There's no one here, I'm not in danger, I need to sleep!* she huffs to herself, knowing that she needs to get back to sleep before the soldiers come back to question her again.

It had only been a few hours since the meat had been brought in. Cleo couldn't tell how much time had passed, but by the fatigue in her limbs and the sleep lingering in the back of her mind, she couldn't have been asleep longer than five hours. Judging by the jitteriness in her limbs though, she knows it will take some time before she is relaxed enough for sleep.

"Might as well work on a few of the bolts," she muses to herself quietly, turning to the metal plate keeping her at the back of her cell. She settles on her knees by the wall, focusing on the upper right bolt this time, reasoning that the right side will be weakened by the fact that she had pulled the lower right bolt out.

When she takes the slightly roughened metal between her left pointer finger and thumb, she eases a nail beneath the small gap between the head of the bolt and the metal plate. Cleo closes her eyes and focuses on her left hand, causing her nail to thicken, sharpen and strengthen between the two metal surfaces.

With a ping, the bolt shoots into her palm and falls to the floor before she can catch it. She opens her eyes and searches the ground, picking out the glinting metal against the dark stone of her cell. She snatches the bolt and pushes it back into place.

Before she can move on to the next corner, the sound of footfalls outside her door breaks into her concentration. Cleo freezes, waiting with bated breath to hear if the footsteps stop or not. To her apprehension, the footsteps stop and the rattle of a key in the lock forces her up onto her feet.

"Stand back!" comes the order as the sliding panel opens, revealing a man's aggressive face. Cleo doesn't move but settles her feet in preparation to move if needed. The door opens and four men and a woman walk in. One man raises his baton but the others leave their weapons in the holsters.

"Take her," the woman orders, gesturing to the two men furthest to her right. To the one with the baton in his hand, she points to Cleo's chest. "Release the chest strap. The Colonel wants her moved."

No! the Alpha voice in Cleo's head snarls. *All our work will be for nothing! We can't be moved!*

A growl escapes Cleo's mouth without her permission as the men grab her wrists and latch wide manacles just above their hands. Each man holds each of her arms along with the restraints. The baton wielding man steps around to her back and with a few quick movements with a key later, Cleo sighs unconsciously in relief as the straps fall away.

"Wrap her up," the woman commands, handing the man a length of white cloth. He takes it, wrapping it swiftly across Cleo's chest.

Get your hands off me! the Alpha snarls, watching the man through Cleo's eyes. *You great pervert! Get your filthy hands off!*

Shut the fuck up! Cleo must scream to the voice, mentally shoving it back into the recesses of her mind again. *I need to focus!* She grits her teeth as the cloth is tightened swiftly and the soldier backs away.

"Follow me, monster." The woman turns and marches out into the hall. One of the other soldiers follows before the two men holding Cleo shove their captive forward.

Catching herself before she falls forward, Cleo manages to walk with the men, their progress slightly hampered in the doorway by the necessity of one of the men going through first before walking her sideways through the portal and into a hallway. The woman marches ahead, moving toward a staircase at the end of the wall leading further down into the building. The soldiers follow the trio of Cleo and her guards and shut the door behind them.

"Keep moving!" the man on her right orders as Cleo glances behind her. Cleo bites back the retort and continues to follow the woman down the hall. As the trio walks down the stairs, she notices that the walls are a lot thicker and the halls quite a bit narrower than those of the floor above. The woman turns left at the bottom of the steps and down another hall. To her left, she stops about three-quarters of the way down the hall at another thick metal door and unlocks it, the rust on the hinges causing it to squeal when it opens halfway. Cleo winces at the shrill noise and stumbles in her momentary hesitation.

As if feeling her stumble was a sign of refusal to follow, the men on either side of her shove her forcefully forward with unnecessary violence through the old door. Once inside, they roughly force her arms above her head and latch a metal device to her arms, keeping them locked tight together. Cleo hears the rattle of chains, and her arms are stretched upwards, pulling her body weight uncomfortably off her feet to the point where she is struggling to maintain her balance on her toes to avoid stretching her shoulders and arms. The woman stalks in front of Cleo, watching as she fights to find her footing.

"My name is Captain Lews," the woman says, beginning to pace back and forth in the narrow confines of the room in front of Cleo. "I am here to ask you questions. I expect you to answer them and give me as much information as you can."

"Yes, Captain," Cleo grunts, knowing the woman is expecting a response to her words. "I will answer."

You should keep your mouth shut. the Alpha snarls from its corner in her brain. *They'll leave you up here for days and you'll never get out.* Cleo shakes herself mentally, pulling her focus back to the captain in front of her.

"Where did you get bitten?" Captain Lews asks, not watching Cleo's discomfort.

"On my shoulder," Cleo grunts, shrugging her left shoulder. "There should be a scar and everything. I didn't realize what had happened at the time. I was more focused on getting my friends out of trouble."

"Where were you bitten geographically?" the captain demands. "If large numbers of Lycans are in the area, we need to be aware and we need to take steps to prevent others from meeting the same fate."

"I don't remember," Cleo whines, her toes becoming uncomfortable after the few moments being stuck in the awkward position. Her shoulders too had begun to ache sharply. "It was over two weeks ago. I don't know exactly where we were, but we were in a forest just outside of a ruined city."

"How did you learn how to look human? No other Lycan we've ever seen has been able to appear as human as you do." The captain pauses in her pacing to look Cleo up and down if incredulous at Cleo's audacity to look normal when she clearly wasn't.

"No one taught me anything," Cleo whimpers, struggling to ease the tension in her back. "I didn't want to be a monster. I figured out how to be human on my own. I don't want to be a monster! I never knew what I was doing! I wanted to be normal."

The captain scoffs at this explanation before moving on. "Who knows you've transformed? Certainly, your friends knew something of what had happened. They've been traveling with you for so long. They must have noticed that you were changing."

"Only Elijah knows," Cleo says shortly. "I disappeared from my group for a few days when I started to change. I explained after I had disappeared that I had been found by a small settlement when I had collapsed during hunting and the settlement had taken me in to help me heal."

"But there was no settlement?" the woman guesses unconcernedly.

"No. I just tailed my friends at a distance until I could control myself," Cleo explains, omitting meeting her father, Themis, and Zoya, knowing that the thought of Lycans anywhere near the settlement would start a panic and the three would be in danger. "I returned to them after a few days, realizing it was just in my head. I could become human if I wanted to."

The captain's eyes narrow as she continues to pace, but she doesn't comment on what Cleo says. She continues her questioning. "When did Elijah find out what you are?"

Cleo flinches at the use of the word "what" but answers all the same. "He found out only the day before you lot captured me."

"How did he find out?"

"He followed me after dinner that evening," Cleo says, panting now at the effort to keep her weight off her shoulders. "I had gotten some raw meat after my hunt that day and was planning on eating it in an abandoned building. He followed me and walked in after I had transformed to eat."

"Have you bitten anyone else?" The question comes suddenly and Captain Lews turns to face Cleo straight on as she asks it.

The bitch is suspicious, the Alpha rumbles almost satisfied at the question. *Doesn't like to think about you walking around, free to bite any of her precious humans.* Cleo internally groans at the Alpha before answering.

"I've never bitten anyone," she states baldly. "I told you. I want to be human. I have never lost control and attacked anyone. I am perfectly capable of controlling myself."

The captain searches Cleo's face for a long moment before turning away. The soldiers precede her out the door, but she pauses when Cleo says, "Wait!" Cleo struggles to maintain her footing. "Let me down!"

The captain scoffs a laugh before leaving, the loud click of the lock throwing Cleo into fresh panic.

We're going to die chained to the ceiling. The Omega, who had until this point remained silent, pokes its head out of its dark corner, the panic in its thoughts permeating all of Cleo's senses, making the pain and fear more intense. *They're never going to let us out of this! We're going to hang here until we suffocate!*

Cleo lets out a growl of frustration, letting her head hang on her chest to loosen the muscles of her back. After a few seconds, she begins to search her surroundings. In front of her, the door looms too far and out of any hope of reach. *As if I don't have enough to worry about without dangling from the ceiling, risking ripping up my shoulders, but I can't do anything to help any of my friends or myself.*

You should have given them a different answer, the Omega whimpers. *They wanted a different answer.*

"There weren't any other answers I could have given," Cleo mutters aloud, frustrated with the multitude of voices in her head.

The hours pass achingly slow as Cleo half hangs in her restraints. Intermittently, her legs collapse beneath her, leaving her to hang from her wrists. At first, the hanging allows her legs to rest; after a few moments, however, the pressure of her body weight pulling on her shoulders causes her breath to catch as she is unable to completely expand her chest. Her shortness of breath forces her to wake from her stupor to get her feet beneath her again.

This cycle repeats itself several times over the nearly twelve hours between the soldiers chaining her to the ceiling and the captain returning.

The captain strides forward, startling Cleo who hadn't heard the officer enter the room. In her right hand, a long rod with a two-pronged tip waves gently with her footsteps.

"Good morning." The captain's voice drips with sarcasm. "Did you sleep well?" Without waiting for Cleo's response, she jabs the rod at Cleo's left leg.

A sharp jolt of electricity lances into the muscle of her thigh, causing Cleo to shriek in pain and surprise. Once the rod is removed, the pain fades quickly. The captain begins to circle her, the rod kept near Cleo's skin.

"Where did you get bitten?" the captain demands, watching Cleo closely. Cleo huffs in her restraints.

"I told you this already," she groans. "I was bitten on the shoulder and didn't realize I had been bitten. It happened over a week and a half ago in a wooded area southwest of here.

I don't know exactly where, though I'm sure it's drenched in dried blood after the fight we had."

The captain jabs the rod at Cleo's right side this time, making the prisoner jerk spasmodically and nearly lose her footing as she flinches away from the searing pain.

"Why are you jabbing me?" Cleo bursts out, frustration making her reckless. "I'm telling you the truth!"

"How did you learn how to look human?" the captain demands, ignoring Cleo's outburst.

"I didn't want to be a monster!" Cleo snarls. "No one taught me, as I've told you before. I just wanted to be human."

Again, the prod, this time at her left side, right at the edge of her ribcage. Cleo shrieks incoherently this time, unable to contain herself.

"Who knows what you are?" The captain's questions keep coming immediately after the electrified jabs.

"Only Elijah!" Cleo sobs, prepared for another shock. She tenses, but the jab comes late. Just as she relaxes from the lack of a prod, the jolt comes from directly below her right shoulder blade, the captain continuing to circle Cleo as she asks the questions. Cleo's legs collapse beneath her this time and she hangs from the chains.

"When did Elijah find out?" the captain asks, stepping around to Cleo's face again. Cleo grunts to respond.

"The day before I was captured." Her voice is muffled from the pressure on her shoulders, neck, and chest. "He followed me after dinner. I didn't realize he would find me and follow me. I thought I had found a secluded spot to eat." Again, the jolt comes right beneath her left shoulder blade.

Cleo stands in an uncontrolled jerk as electricity courses through her body again, but this time, she doesn't make a sound.

"Have you bitten anyone else?" The captain's voice is right in Cleo's left ear this time.

"No." Cleo's vehement hiss holds venom, as if wishing she could give a different answer. A flash of white-hot pain lances from the base of Cleo's skull and then blackness consumes her.

*   *   *

Colonel Rhys Griffin stares avidly at the scene unfolding on the opposite side of the window in front of him. Cleo, who had previously been standing precariously on her toes with her arms taut from the strain of being held above her head, convulsed horribly the instant the cattle prod touched the base of her skull. When the prod is removed, she falls limp hanging from her chained wrists. For a split second, Griffin senses something is wrong, but no one moves. And then, all hell breaks loose.

Cleo wrenches her arms from the ceiling, the chain links splitting like paper. Her body contorts, changing from the human shape a moment before to a more animalistic form. Her legs bunch up, the muscles growing and thickening while her torso hunches. Her hands and feet become more paw-like with sharp, lengthening claws. Her face narrows and elongates to more of a snout.

Unaware of the sudden danger because of her awkward view, the captain jabs the cattle prod into Cleo's exposed side, yelling about how the Lycan had freed herself. Cleo moves almost faster than the eye can follow. She rips her arms apart, then grabs the captain's shoulder with claws and fangs, shaking her like a rag doll before throwing the limp and bleeding body to the floor.

A private who had been standing beside the door runs forward, a baton raised in his left fist. Cleo closes the distance between them with a single bound before ripping the soldier's arm off at the shoulder. The man shrieks before Cleo tears out his throat.

"Send them in," the colonel barks, not moving his eyes from the window. "Four darts should be sufficient." *Two darts would be enough to fell a horse,* he muses to himself as gun-toting soldiers enter the room two by two. *Surely four can drop this beast.*

The first two men each get off a shot, drawing the Lycan's attention from the ravaged corpse. The second two through the door loose their shots as she snarls at the approaching figures.

Cleo stands but sways as she takes a step toward the threat to her meal. An instant later, she collapses to the blood-puddled floor. Her body slowly returns to its human form with slight differences. Instead of smooth, bare skin, the thick fur that had covered her bestial form had thinned to resemble more of a fine down instead of a pelt. Her face keeps a slightly narrower appearance while still maintaining mostly human features.

Colonel Griffin moves from the window, joining the five other soldiers in the hall. He pauses at the door as two medics rush through to check on the captain and private. After the medics pass, Griffin enters and glances around the room at the carnage left by Cleo's rampage. Already a medic is pulling a sheet over the mauled private, but two others work quickly beside the captain.

"Stabilize her, then take her to one of the Lycan cells," the colonel orders. "I want detailed notes on her condition. Please keep me informed with regular reports."

"Yes, sir," the medics reply immediately.

Griffin turns to the Lycan lying on the floor. The soldiers who had dropped her stand guard with weapons drawn, as if expecting her to rise at any moment.

"I want the thickest, strongest chains we have," Griffin orders one of the soldiers. "Bring manacles for her, and we'll get her restrained again. I don't want anyone to work with her. We'll let her wake up on her own. I want hourly reports on her status."

"Yes, sir." The remaining soldiers salute and rush to follow his commands. Griffin stays to ensure Cleo is taken care of appropriately, then orders some raw meat to be left in the cell with a basin of water.

Can't let her die of dehydration, Griffin muses. *Though I think we should leave the mess she made. Give her a little bit to worry about.*

"Don't mop up," he tells his subordinates scurrying around him. "Leave the blood. You can take away the body, but the blood should stay."

At the following nods, the colonel turns for the door, trusting in his underlings to follow through with his orders.

*   *   *

A heart-wrenching shriek rents the air, startling Themis so badly, he drops from his bunk as he is climbing into the bed. His legs buckle and he sprawls on the floor. He sees Abrahm look over the side of the lower bunk at him.

"Who—?" Themis begins, glancing up, but trails off at the frustrated shake of the other Alpha's head. Themis finds his footing, watching his mentor close his eyes, brow furrowed. Themis takes a breath, slowing his racing heart and pauses to ponder what had happened. As he turns inward, the sense of unbridled panic returns vaguely but more animalistic than before.

"They're trying to break her." Abrahm's voice is tight and angry, hushed because of the men sleeping in the other beds at the end of the room. "Your head okay?" He looks to Themis.

"Yeah." Themis scrubs his right hand through the hair on the back of his skull. "What was that?"

"Cleo." Abrahm moves to stand from his bunk. "She doesn't know what she's doing, but she's reaching out blindly for any help she can get. They're torturing her and if they don't stop soon, they're risking bringing an army of Omegas to their gates."

"What do you mean?" Themis glances around at the sleeping men.

"That shriek that startled you out of bed probably reached every Lycan in about a ten-to-fifteen-mile radius, if not further." Abrahm follows Themis's glance and shrugs. "They'll likely all be called to fight unless the people in charge stop torturing her."

"Can you find her?" Themis wonders aloud, returning his gaze to Abrahm. "Can you use her call to narrow in on her location from here?"

"Yes," Abrahm murmurs. "I have a direction, and I'm pretty sure that if I really tried, I could narrow it down more." He looks to the darkened window. "But I don't want to go into the streets until morning. There's a curfew and I don't want to get shot on sight."

"Agreed." Themis nods. "But I don't like thinking about Cleo stuck in pain for any longer than she has been. She's been through enough."

"Go to bed," Abrahm recommends. "We'll go looking for her as soon as we get up." Abrahm nods to the bed above him. "No sense worrying until we can actually do something for her."

Themis nods in agreement and scrambles up to his bunk. It takes him longer than usual to fall asleep, the sense of panic that had filled him still lingering in the back of his mind. When he finally falls asleep, visions of Cleo trapped in a cage haunt him through the night.

An hour or two after dawn, Themis sits up when he feels Abrahm moving beneath him. The two Alphas dress quietly and slip out of the dormitory before the other men even stir. The crisp morning air clears Themis's worries more than

Abrahm's reassuring words of the night before. Beside him, Abrahm stalks slowly, a look of deep concentration on his face. Unsure of the requirements to find Cleo's mental call, Themis stays a pace or two behind Abrahm to keep out of the way.

If it weren't a matter of life or death, I'd be determined to learn what he is doing, Themis thinks to himself. *When we get Cleo free, I'll make sure to learn.*

She's in there. Abrahm's voice in his head makes Themis jump as they both look at the imposing structure. *She's under the ground, thickly muffled by stone and metal, but she's there.*

Abrahm takes them south and west of the building where their dormitory had been held. This early in the morning, only soldiers finishing up their night's watch walk the streets, looking more interested in finding their beds than in the men walking with them. Themis notices Abrahm narrow his eyes at a large dark building directly west from where they stand, pausing as if to ascertain they had gone the correct direction.

How will we get her out of there? Themis asks silently to his partner as they cross a thoroughfare to get a closer look. *It must be a prison. I'm sure there are guards and other dangers we'll need to figure out.*

"Excuse me," Abrahm calls to a woman soldier standing at the corner of a building nearby. She looks up at him, a polite smile on her face. "Could you tell me what that building is? We're new to the settlement and we wanted to get our bearings."

"Of course, sir." The woman nods. "That's the Southern Quarter's containment block." At their questioning frowns she continues. "That's where the army holds all of the people arrested in the Southern Quarter of the settlement. It's run by Colonel Rhys Griffin."

"Thank you." Abrahm smiles at her and they turn back to their dormitory. "You've been exceedingly helpful." The woman smiles at them as they walk away and returns to her post. Themis glances at Abrahm covertly.

What are we doing now? he demands of the elder Alpha. *We know where she's at. Why don't we just go in there, get her and get out?*

We will. Abrahm reassures Themis, but Themis can hear the slight impatience in the tone. *But we need more information. I want to talk to Charlie and see what information he can gather before we try anything. It wouldn't help us if we managed to get in but were killed before we could get Cleo out.*

Themis sighs and they continue on their way.

*   *   *

Abrahm scans the area around the containment block. He had left Themis at the barracks to look for Charlie and to go over any new information Charlie might have found before coming back to scope out the square around the Southern Quarter Containment Block.

The square seems to be a meeting grounds of sorts for the garrison of soldiers in this part of the settlement. Men and women in matted green and mud brown meet to converse in the shade of the building. Many pass through the doors, and several times as he watches, Abrahm notices people with armbands of white with red crosses rush through as if called on important business.

Abrahm also notes the different streets that lead to and from the building. This containment center appears to have been built at the crossroads of a central point in the old city that used to be here. The roads branch off in six of the major cardinal directions. Abrahm notes the western-most street appears the least populated and least used of all of them. He moves along the edge of the square and passes into the western road without issue.

His bearing mimics that of the soldiers he passes. With his back straight and a look of concentration on his face, no one stops him. As he walks, he makes note of the changing landscape. The further he goes out from the center the fewer buildings appear to be used. Instead of one in three doors being boarded up, it becomes more like one in ten doors that look used. The walls facing the street begin to look as though they have been half-demolished and left to weather away. Strips of jagged sheet metal litter the alleyways between buildings and only the odd straggler appears to use the road as Abrahm approaches the perimeter wall.

The wall looms ahead, a vast patchwork of sheet metal, wood, and stone put up when the first hordes of Lycans began showing up and attacking people. Abrahm knows from his and Themis's scouting before Cleo's capture that there are guard towers spaced at rough intervals along the wall to watch for approaching Lycans, but he doesn't see one directly before him.

Good, he muses, scanning the road before him and making calculations. *The less we're seen, the better.* Ahead, in the nine or so feet between the end of the rows of buildings and the wall, sheets of scrap metal, barbed wire, and large rusting caltrops nearly cover the ground. There is a path of sorts that leads close to the wall where a sheet of metal appears to be loosely attached to the rest of the framework monstrosity.

Abrahm walks forward but turns to ensure his approach isn't observed. No one walks up the western road that he can see, so he approaches the mulch of debris from the wall and years of neglect. As he gets within about five feet of the wall, he spots the watchtowers on either side of him. One rises about ten feet to his right, the other about twenty feet to his left. Neither side has a door down at Abrahm's level, so he assumes they enter from other towers and walk the catwalks above to reach the tower posts. From his position more than fifteen feet below the crest of the wall, Abrahm can't see the guards if they are posted but he reasons if he can't see them, they can't see him.

Abrahm moves carefully, stepping around the sharp metal scraps, and makes it to a small, cleared space directly beside the wall. The crimped, slightly rusted sheet of metal sheeting before him seems to only have one bolt still fastening it to the wall. He pushes it gently to the side and the four-foot-tall sheet slides almost soundlessly up to reveal a hole through the wall.

We have our way out. He sighs with relief before returning the sheet back to its original position. Instead of clearing the path to this hidden escape route, Abrahm leaves it, relying on the scattered mess of debris to hide its location until it's needed.

*   *   *

The metallic taste of blood on her tongue throws Cleo out of her sleepy stupor more forcefully and completely than a bomb going off next to her ear. She sits bolt upright and immediately spits out the remaining saliva in her mouth. When that doesn't remove the taste, bile rises in the back of her throat.

What did you do? She mentally rounds on the Alpha sitting proudly at the entrance to her corner of Cleo's mind.

I took control. Alpha's tone is smug. *You dropped away and I took control for us. I set us free.*

Cleo glances down at her wrists. Heavy manacles circle her wrists and ankles, then turns inward.

We don't look free, she snarls, rattling the metal to prove her point. *I still see chains.*

We're not hanging from the ceiling, Alpha sneers. *This is an improvement.*

What did you do? Cleo demands again. *Why is there blood all over me?*

We ripped into a few humans, Alpha practically sings. *They tried to punish us for being who we are. I taught them to truly fear us.*

Did we eat anyone? Cleo growls, dreading the answer but desperate to hear it.

Hell if I know. Alpha's sheer disregard angers Cleo beyond endurance. She stands, intending to pace the blood-spattered cell. She manages to get but two or three paces in any direction. The manacles chafe her wrists and Alpha moves to take control. She snarls in frustration as Cleo cuts her off.

You've done enough! she explodes at the wolf in her. *Shut up and let me try to repair the damage you've caused.* She turns to the mirrored window.

Before she can call out, multiple pairs of footsteps echo in the hall beyond the door to her prison. A key clicks in the lock and Colonel Griffin marches in, flanked by two soldiers.

He's not happy with you. The Omega pokes its nose out of its corner. *Don't let him hurt us,* it begs. Cleo shakes her head slightly to clear it before looking up at the colonel.

"I'm sorry for what happened." Cleo adopts a submissive demeanor despite Alpha lunging for control again. "I didn't mean to lose control."

"Your regret doesn't change what happened." The colonel sniffs, regarding her coolly. "I've lost two good soldiers to you. I didn't come here to listen to your mewling."

Alpha's hackles raise and Cleo feels herself bristling despite her efforts to cool the rage boiling within her. She glances at the two soldiers accompanying the colonel and then bows her head both to display the sincerity of her words and to disguise the fire in her eyes.

"I'm sorry about your men." She is happy to hear her voice is calm and contrite. "I didn't want to kill anyone. I lost control, but I can assure you I have regained and intend to maintain control on the wilder side of myself."

"That's good to hear," Colonel Griffin replies. "Though I will reserve my judgment until I have seen it for myself." He looks her up and down as if measuring her. "Do you have any questions?" he asks, his voice cold and uncaring.

Cleo takes a deep breath and looks up. "I want to leave," she states boldly. "I want to leave the settlement. I hold no grudge against you or the people living here. I will not seek revenge, but—" before she can finish her statement, Griffin holds up a hand.

"You are a prisoner," he says, his voice impassive. "You are not at liberty to leave. You are to be held until a trial can be had for your crimes against the settlement."

"Crimes against the settlement?" The words blurt from her mouth without her consent as the Alpha roars her displeasure. Before Cleo can regain control, the Alpha continues. "You are holding me against my will, torturing me for information I've already given you! I ought to kill every one of you!"

Colonel Griffin's face hardens, but a glint in his eye tells Cleo he had expected her reaction and it was exactly what he wanted. He turns to the door.

"Bring him in." The words are unexpected and shocks the Alpha enough for Cleo to gain control again. She mentally shoves Alpha back to her corner of the mind and tries to think of who the colonel might have brought. Her jaw drops as a nearly unrecognizable figure is shoved into the cell to collapse at Colonel Griffin's feet.

The figure on the floor is barely able to move from his half-crouched slump on the stone floor. He struggles to get upright, moving slowly as if to make sure his movements won't cause more pain. As he lifts his head, Cleo can barely see his normal skin color because of all the mottled bruising. Black and purple blotches interspersed with yellow and green mar the puffy skin, showing places where the man had been hit multiple times at different times.

He grins when he spots Cleo, and she sees the bloody stumps of broken teeth. A cut above his left eye weeps blood while on his right cheek there's a mixture of blood and pus. Gazing closer at the face before her, Cleo gasps.

"Elijah!" She almost darts forward, brought up short by the chains binding her to the floor. She stands, two feet from the unrecognizable figure. "Elijah, what happened to you?"

Colonel Griffin answers. "Elijah here has discovered the rewards of aiding the settlement in its quest to discover and capture Lycans." His tone is light, but his eyes shoot daggers at the cowering man before him. "Haven't you, Eli?"

Eli's neck contracts between his shoulders as he peers up at the colonel through heavily slitted eyes. "Yes," he squeaks, eyes darting away from the colonel quickly. The skin around his eyes is so swollen it is a wonder to Cleo how he can see at all.

She takes a deep breath and mentally wrestles the Alpha into a cage at the back of her mind, her own anger fueling her strength and determination to beat the colonel.

"I'll do whatever you want, just leave him alone!" Cleo yells, only preventing herself from charging against her bonds by the barest hint of mental control. The colonel scoffs and kicks out at Elijah, catching the cowering prisoner in the chest with the toe of his boot. Cleo hears muffled crunches and an abrupt shift in Eli's breathing.

"Colonel Griffin!" A private bursts into the cell, out of breath. "Colonel! Commander Ebrose sent me! There is a situation at the wall. Commander Ebrose requires you to man your station!"

At the private's interruption, Cleo's world freezes. One look at Eli is enough to confirm her in the knowledge of his imminent death. Griffin's kick had likely broken several ribs which in turn had punctured his lung.

You've got nothing left to lose, Alpha growls from her corner. *You can't save him. You can surrender and die in chains, or you can try to escape and risk dying free.*

Griffin turns his attention to the intrusion quickly. "What's happening, Private?"

With the colonel distracted, Cleo takes a step backwards and curls her body in on herself. She closes her eyes and takes a deep breath, ignoring the voices around her momentarily.

You'd better be ready for a fight, she hisses at Alpha who stalks forward at Cleo's motion. *We're getting out of here, but we're doing this together.*

"Lycans, sir!" The private's cry breaks through Cleo's internal preparations. "Lycans are swarming around the southern border! Commander Ebrose wants to ensure that we are prepared if they attack!"

Cleo rolls her shoulders, preparing to shift as Griffin motions to the other soldiers.

"Very well, Private—" Before Colonel Griffin can finish his thought, Cleo springs forward, transforming as she flies forward at the closest guard and shattering the chains restraining her. He fumbles with his weapon as her elongated arm wraps around his throat and twists to break his neck. Using her momentum, she flings herself sideways to avoid the first shots of the second soldier.

Out of the corner of her eye, she sees the private and colonel rushing out the door. Cleo bull rushes the firing man and knocks him sprawling into the wall, headfirst. He stops moving and Cleo turns to race after Colonel Griffin. In the hall, she spots the two men rushing down toward a set of stairs. The private lags, struggling to keep up with his superior despite his obvious panic and incomprehension of the events. Cleo catches him in three bounds of her powerful legs, knocking him senseless with a powerful blow. She hardly breaks stride.

Rhys Griffin glances behind him as he hauls himself up the first four steps as the private collapses. He makes it barely two more steps before Cleo's jaws clamp around the back of his neck.

With a horrible wrench, she breaks his neck and lets him fall from her mouth, disgusted but pleased.

Eli! the Omega's voice whines plaintively, reminding her of her friend. In human form, she races back to find him barely moving.

"Cleo?" He stirs at the darkening of her shadow falling on him. He turns to look up at her. Blood dribbles from the corner of his mouth. He coughs and the wet sound sends a thrill of terror up Cleo's spine.

"I'm here." Tears well at the edge of Cleo's eyes as she lays a gentle hand against Eli's swollen face. "I'm right here. What can I do?"

"I'm sorry." His voice is weak, broken by wracking coughs, each one driving a dagger into Cleo's heart. "I tried to warn you," he gasps in pain as he shifts toward her. "I wanted you to get away."

"It's not your fault." Cleo hushes him, her voice close to breaking. "I should never have tried to pull off being human. I should have left you guys when I had the chance."

Eli groans as he shakes his head and tries to sit up. Cleo presses his shoulder back to the ground and he lacks the strength to fight her.

"You should get out of here." Elijah coughs. "Get out while everyone is gone." He attempts to wipe the blood away from his face, but his hand makes it only halfway to his mouth before falling to his chest. Cleo wipes it away with the ball of her thumb, a tear rolling down her nose and dropping onto his cheek.

"I can't leave you." Her throat constricts with restrained sobs. "You've got to come with me." A single bark of laughter starts Eli to coughing. He gasps and it takes him a minute to get his breath back enough to speak again.

"I think it's a little late for that." He groans with the effort of speaking. "Go. I'll only slow you down." His voice begins to fade. "Kick some ass for me." His laugh is a final sigh and his movements stop. Cleo closes her eyes and allows herself a moment to sob over her friend's cooling body.

Cleo! A new voice in her head makes her start and look up a few moments later. *Cleo! You need to get out! You need to get out now!* The voice is familiar, but no one joins her in the room.

Abrahm? She thinks in her head, hardly daring to believe. *Abrahm, is that you?*

Yes. Abrahm's voice is hard but familiar. *Themis and I are waiting for you outside. You need to get out of the building, and we need to go!*

Everyone should be gone, Abrahm assures her as she turns back to her fallen friend. Without pausing to think about what she is doing, Cleo kneels and slings Eli's body over her shoulders and heads through the door.

*   *   *

The two Lycans trot through the suddenly swarming streets of the city, heading toward the containment block. Soldiers and civilians alike rush past, too focused on their individual tasks to worry about two more bodies in the seething mass of humanity. Abrahm must catch Themis's arm as a group of about six men attempt to push their way between them.

She's coming. Abrahm glances to Themis before indicating they should move closer to a building to avoid being separated by the throngs surrounding them. Themis nods and they press their backs against the building across the thoroughfare from the containment building. As they move along beside the rough stone of the building, Abrahm spots a familiar figure rushing up to them, a loaded pack on his back.

"Have you heard what's happening?" Charlie asks them as he nears, his face tight with anxiety. "Have you had a chance to figure out how to get Cleo out of wherever she is being held?"

Abrahm pulls him out of the suffocating crowds. "Cleo's free and should be coming out of that building very soon." He points to the now-deserted containment block before them. "I have a way out of the settlement, but we need to make sure we aren't spotted."

"In this mayhem?" Charlie asks, looking around, the people finding their way to the battlements of the settlement or into bunkers scattered through the town. "Fat chance."

"She'll be fully transformed," Abrahm corrects Charlie's line of thinking. Charlie gapes at him in astonishment. And Abrahm chuckles at him. "She's breaking her way out of a prison block. You didn't expect her to do that as a human, did you?"

Charlie shrugs defensively before turning his attention to the building. "So, you guys have a plan?" He shifts the pack restlessly on his back.

"As soon as we get word Cleo is coming out of the door, we will start to run," Abrahm continues. "We'll head west. There's a blind spot where I've made an exit of sorts. But we need to move fast. The sooner we get out of here the better."

"I want to come with you," Charlie demands. Themis and Abrahm share a look Charlie catches and he immediately continues. "I want to protect my sister. There's nothing else here for me. Mandi's given us up for dead at this point and I can't find Elijah. Cleo is the last person I have. I'm protecting her."

Cleo will skin us alive. Themis's thought to Abrahm almost makes the older Lycan laugh as he thinks about how furious Cleo will be if they allow her younger brother to come with her, but Abrahm knows how Charlie feels. Being alone is a hard existence.

"Would you be willing to accept all the conditions we place on you once we get you out of here?" Abrahm asks. Charlie doesn't hesitate.

"I will do anything you tell me." Abrahm can hear sincerity in this human's voice. "Just get us both out of here."

Abrahm nods, then glances up. Cleo's thoughts reach him, and he knows his daughter is close to breaking free.

"Let's get ready to go." He looks around the building, glad most humans have disappeared. *We're all clear,* he projects to Cleo, letting her know she can come out of the building. *We're ready to run. Follow Themis and me.* He doesn't add the fact of Charlie's decision to join them. Cleo will be worried about too many other things to add to her plate.

The three men watch as the door to the prison bursts open and Cleo's Lycan form barrels out with a bundle over its shoulders. Without thinking, Abrahm guides his new pack through the now deserted streets to the western wall of the settlement.

The four dash forward, intent on getting to the west wall as quickly as possible. The few people in the streets with them are so intent on reaching their defensive positions they hardly notice the three Lycans and human in their midst. Cleo seems to run with the singlemindedness of escape without noticing her surroundings. She follows Abrahm with little difficulty despite her burden.

When they reach the wall between two tall guard posts, Abrahm guides them through a disguised path through jagged metal and debris to a sheet of rippled metal with one corner bolted to the wall. He pushes the metal up and reveals a hole large enough for them to escape through to the trees beyond. As Cleo stops to take a breath, she glances at Abrahm, Themis, and finally Charlie. Her wolfish features contort in confusion and she growls at her brother.

"He's coming with us, Cleo." Abrahm doesn't bother translating, knowing time is of the essence. *"Don't argue, just go through. Head west. We need to get a few miles away from here before we can talk."*

Cleo gives Abrahm one last hard look before ducking through the wound in the wall. Abrahm catches the scent of human blood as she passes him and realizes she is carrying a corpse. Unable to consider the matter further, he motions Charlie and Themis through after her. He follows and they rush west without a backwards glance at the settlement.

*   *   *

"What do you mean, you're coming with us?" Cleo's sharp voice cuts through the abandoned forest around the six figures. Cleo bears down on her little brother sitting on a boulder covered with moss. He glares right back at his sister without flinching. "How can you be so reckless?"

She's just upset because of everything that's happened, Charlie thinks to himself. *We just buried Eli and Mandi's abandoned us. She doesn't want to see me killed.* He holds up a hand at her, cutting her off so he can speak.

"You're all I've got left, Cleo." His voice is rough but thankfully doesn't break. "I wasn't losing you to the unknown. If you left, I knew I wanted to be there with you."

"But you're not a Lycan!" Cleo cuts in. "You're in danger every minute you're out of the settlement. There's a huge pack of Omegas out here."

"That huge pack of Omegas is currently attempting to rip apart the settlement I was supposed to have stayed in," Charlie reminds her. "Had I stayed I would have been at even greater risk than I am here."

Abrahm had told them about Cleo's Alpha Command to every Omega in the area to attack the settlement. Cleo hadn't removed the command from the beasts and now none of them knew what the result of the attack was.

"You're still human," Cleo protests. "You'll draw Omegas to us, and you'll constantly be in danger."

"Not if you turn me," Charlie murmurs, hardly daring to voice the thought, but each of the Lycans present had heard him. Cleo turns her back on him and walks away.

"I couldn't do that," she says flatly. She doesn't look at the others. "I won't do that."

Zoya steps forward from where she had been lurking. "Of the four of us here, three of us are Alphas." She looks directly at Cleo with defiance. "A bite from an Alpha would give him the best chance to become a Beta like me. But only

Cleo could give him the chance to be an Alpha. As a Master, she is the most powerful of the four of us. If he wants to risk becoming one of us, her bite will give him the best chance at retaining some semblance of his previous life."

Charlie nods, glancing at Cleo. "There is no way I can do this journey as a human." He aims his words at her. "I am making this choice of my own free will. I want to join you, Cleo. I want to help you and I want to protect you. You're my sister. It's my job as your brother to protect you."

She turns to meet his eye, then lowers her gaze. "I don't want you to hate me for turning you into something we've grown up hating."

"You'll be there to help me through the whole thing." Charlie grins at her. He can see the self-loathing in her body language and knows, despite having come to grips with her new reality, she still has miles of work to do before she can completely forgive herself for what has happened.

Cleo sighs, meets Themis's eye and then Charlie's again before stepping back into the group. "Fine. Let's get this over with." She looks to Abrahm. "Where should I bite him?"

"Best place to get him to transform quickly would likely be shoulder or neck." Abrahm studies Charlie critically. "You'll want to give a sharp bite either at his shoulder blade or jugular. You need to pierce but not completely sever one of his main blood vessels."

Charlie jerks in surprise at his words. "What do you mean, main blood vessels?"

"She needs to infect your blood," Abrahm explains. "She needs to get her saliva into your blood so you will transform quickly." He points to Charlie's collarbone. "There is a blood vessel directly behind this bone that is rather large and will help pump her saliva through your body quickly. This will help the transformation happen quickly, over one day instead of three."

Cleo takes a deep breath, then rolls her neck and transforms. Even after seeing her transformed once before, Charlie finds having her wolf-like snout inches from his throat makes him gulp involuntarily. He steadies himself with a deep breath and closes his eyes.

"Gently, Cleo," Abrahm instructs, marking the spot on Charlie's collarbone with a small scratch of his nail. "Just here."

And with enormous restraint and focus, Cleo's teeth puncture Charlie's skin. The pain is less than he had expected, judging on the power behind Cleo's jaws, and Charlie barely whimpers as Cleo backs away swiftly. Abrahm presses a rag firmly against the wound, his pressure causing the wound to ache more than the initial puncture.

"Here." Themis passes a newly transformed Cleo a waterskin. She takes a swig, swishes it around her mouth, and spits it out violently. Charlie watches her repeat this process two more times before she takes a gulp and swallows.

"I'm never biting you again," she says vehemently, glaring at her brother. Abrahm chuckles at this before looking down at the wound as he removes the rag from Charlie's shoulder.

"You won't have to," he says, wiping a small trickle of blood from Charlie's skin. "Let's settle down for the night and we can determine our plan in the morning."

The group of six start gathering their packs to set up a small camp and settle into the familiar routine of camping.

*   *   *

He's going to hate you. The snarl in her head brings Cleo back to full consciousness again. She sighs and sits up. Night still settles around the campsite as she moves to crawl out of her sleeping bag. There would be no sleep tonight.

"You okay?" Themis murmurs from his position near the fire, clearly still half asleep. Cleo waves for him to go back to sleep and moves toward where she knows Abrahm sits, keeping second watch.

He's going to hate you for turning you into the same monster as you, the Alpha's voice nags at her and Cleo mentally shakes herself.

He's my brother! she snaps back at the furious creature. *He asked me to change him to keep us all safe. Now shut up!*

As she approaches him, she sees Abrahm studying her. His eyes are kind and understanding as she settles beside him without speaking. At first, he simply lets her sit in quiet. His presence soothes her somewhat, knowing he is there to help her. As she settles in, he speaks gently.

"She's wrong, you know." His words make her start and turn to him. He smiles gently at her. "Your wolf. She's wrong. Charlie won't hate you. He won't struggle alone like you had to."

"What do you mean, my wolf?" Cleo asks, confused and wrong-footed.

"That voice in your head," he murmurs, keeping his voice low to prevent the others from hearing and waking up. "She's your wolf. Well, one of them." He chuckles darkly. "You have two, but one is usually very quiet and only comes out when you meet a more powerful Alpha." He studies her eyes. "You've heard more from yours because of what they did to you."

"Why didn't you tell me about them?" Cleo asks, struggling to come to grips with the news that she wasn't going crazy. "I thought all this time that there was something wrong with me! They've been driving me mad since I went into the Settlement."

"I forgot to mention it." Abrahm sighs. "I've never had to explain becoming an Alpha to anyone. We've all just grown up with our wolves. They are a part of us. We grow up talking to them, learning from them. They help quicken our transformations and ease our qualms about eating people."

"Why is mine so out of control?" Cleo asks as the Alpha in her head growls again. "She's constantly yelling at me. It's like having someone else trying to take control of my body all the time."

"I think part of her wildness stems from your own initial refusal of who you are." Abrahm's voice is concerned and grave. "I think when you first started trying to subdue your wolfish instincts, she took it to heart and thought you were trying to kill her. She didn't like it and is now trying to exert control again."

"She's already taken control a few times," Cleo confesses. She tells Abrahm about her experiences being imprisoned in the settlement and about waking up a few times without the memories of how she had become covered in blood. "Last time, I almost couldn't recover control from her."

"It will just take practice," Abrahm reassures her. "She needs to learn that you are both working together. She'll come around. Themis and I will try to help you gain her trust back."

Cleo grins at her father, knowing he will do his best, but her thoughts turn to the strength she feels around the Alpha. The wolf paces in her small corner of Cleo's mind, always on edge and snappish. *She's not likely to trust quickly.* Cleo settles beside Abrahm and slowly falls back to sleep.

The next day, Charlie's fever spikes and he reports his senses have sharpened. Abrahm recommends they break camp and head out in search of some Omegas. On their walk, Cleo chooses to stay beside her brother. They talk about memories of home, about Eli and their friends. Both fall into lapses of silence from time to time and the others leave them to their remembrances. During one of these lapses, Cleo notices Charlie's scent begin to shift. At first, she puts it down to a change in the wind, but soon realizes his scent is stronger, more pungent. She glances over at him and sees beads of sweat running down his cheeks. His whole body trembles like a leaf and he stops walking. Cleo stops with him, raising a hand to prevent the others from speaking.

"Charlie?" she murmurs, her voice gentle and unthreatening. His head snaps up at her words and she sees his eyes flash yellow for a moment. His lip curls in a snarl before his whole body begins to transform. Without thinking, Cleo shrugs into her own transformation.

"Charlie, it's me," she rumbles, ignoring Abrahm, Themis, and Zoya who all transform as well. *"It's Cleo. I'm here to help you."*

"Cleo?" Charlie's growl is tinged with uncertainty as he crouches to spring at her. *"Cleo, what—?"* He lunges forward, but Cleo manages to step aside, shrugging her pack onto the ground and allowing herself to turn fully wolf. She meets Charlie's second lunge with her own, using her superior size and agility to turn her brother where she wants him to go.

Out of the corner of her eye, she sees Themis, Abrahm, and Zoya transform but hesitate to join the fray. Knowing that she will have plenty of support should she need it, Cleo rounds on her brother. Sensing a fight and a potential challenger to her turf, the Alpha comes charging from her corner in Cleo's mind.

Help me tire him out, Cleo offers to the Alpha, bracing herself to give over a modicum of control to the wolf-being inside her. *We need to get him to listen to us.*

The Alpha seems hesitant to take the offered control for a moment and in the distraction of the power shift, Charlie manages to get hold of Cleo's shoulder in his jaws. The pain and jostling jars her to the imminent danger and the two minds of Alpha and Omega meld together.

Before Charlie can get a strong hold on her shoulder with his fangs, Cleo manages to wriggle her right forearm up into Charlie's open mouth and shoves a closed fist nearly into his throat. Startled, he chokes and spits her out, whining in protest at his aching jaw muscles and gagging.

"Don't try to eat me then!" Cleo reprimands with a snarl. *"Listen to me instead."* When he just turns back and charges

again, she swats his face with a stunning forepaw blow to his jaw. She moves gracefully away from his attacks, guiding him in circles, keeping their movement restricted to one area so that their shrieks, growls, and howling wouldn't cause more problems.

Back and forth they battle, pushing and testing each other. Charlie, raw with new power from his first transformation begins to tire as Cleo hits her stride. She matches each of her brother's strikes with ease, only fighting back with the power necessary to keep herself safe. She doesn't want to use her Alpha power unless she needs to. As Charlie begins to calm, she starts pushing him more, able to make him stagger and twice he sits on his haunches, momentarily looking like a dog sitting for a treat before he lies down and shows Cleo his belly in submission.

"Are you ready to listen to me?" she snaps at him, her ears flattening to show her irritation and annoyance. Charlie whines piteously and licks plaintively at her muzzle. *"Okay, listen to me. I need you to think about being human. Think about being Charlie."*

She watches him close his eyes momentarily and nudges him with her muzzle once before she pushes her own transformation back to human form again. When she looks back down, her brother lies at her feet, muddy, tousle-haired, and scared-looking. His eyes flick open and closed rapidly, as if trying to figure out what was going on.

"What happened?" he asks, confused and obviously apprehensive about this new-found side of himself.

"First transformation." Abrahm's voice comes from the trees to Cleo's right as she looks down on her little brother. "You did well. Though I'm thankful that you didn't kill your sister."

Charlie grins nervously up at him, but Cleo offers him a hand and pulls him to his feet. Once she has him standing beside her, she gives him a thorough once-over. She looks closely into his face, then at other parts of his physique before dismissing him with a smile.

"You're fine." She sighs, almost to herself. "No doubt. You're an Alpha." She turns and grins at her father and he can see the relief in her face as she reassures herself that her brother didn't change as much as she thought he might have.

Charlie looks her full in the face and smiles for what seems the first time since they arrived in the Settlement. He gives his sister a full hug, and then looks over at the rest of the Lycans in the area. Their faces fall at the sight of Abrahm's look of hesitation that deepens into a scowl when he moves forward and gives a sniff in Charlie's direction.

"I'm sorry, Cleo," he says, shaking his head lightly. "He's not an Alpha. He's a Beta. He has the scent of one. I think his transformation back into his human form is greatly thanks to your help in teaching him. I'm sure the more he transforms, the less human he will appear. But for the most part, he'll retain his personality." He puts a hand on Cleo's shoulder. "This isn't the optimal outcome, but it's one of the best we could have hoped for."

"What do you mean, he's a Beta?" Cleo demands, looking her brother up and down again. "He looks completely human again."

"It's not something you can necessarily see." Themis steps up behind Abrahm and gives a deep inhale before nodding. "It's a smell. Distinctive between the different ranks, more so than between individual Lycans." He offers his arm to her. "Give me a sniff, then sniff your brother. You'll be able to tell a difference."

Shaking her head in disbelief as she steps forward, Cleo closes her eyes and gives a deep sniff of Themis's wrist. A rich musk of earth, rotting vegetation, and the faint tang of animal blood is there, along with a scent she can't quite place but that smells vaguely familiar and comforting. She opens her eyes, turns back to Charlie and does the same thing to him. This time, the smell is a mix of her brother's fading human scent that she had gotten used to, the earth and vegetation musk, along with a tangier scent that she remembers smelling on Zoya. She frowns and looks up at Charlie.

"I'm sorry, too," she murmurs, then wraps her arms around his neck.

Taken aback by her sudden expression of remorse for something he feels was out of her control, Charlie takes half a step back before giving her a hug back and letting out a chuckle.

"Hell, as long as I'll be safe in this new normal we have to deal with, that is fine with me," he says with confidence. "And I feel fine. No need to fuss, Cleo."

She releases him and gives a slight smile. "Alright." She looks up at the other two men. "Should we get going?"

Abrahm nods and the group continues on.

Over the next few days, they travel west and north. They don't follow any one road but rather just a general route. Themis and Zoya tend to lead, their instinctive sense of home guiding more than anything. Along the way, they see other groups of Lycans. Several have an Alpha or Beta in their midst and those groups often stop Themis and Zoya to ask them what their business is.

Each time they stop, Abrahm chooses to stay back with Cleo and Charlie, encouraging them to take on a more wolfish aspect. The two younger Lycans follow his advice, and after three encounters in one day about a week into their travels, Cleo decides to just keep her wolfish traits when she transforms after eating. Abrahm gives her a wink and follows suit.

"So, what should we expect in this settlement of Lycans?" Cleo asks as they set up camp. "Will we need to do anything special to gain access or anything like that?"

"You'll want to be in your wolf form when we approach," Zoya pipes up before either of the men can say anything. "We'll likely be getting close to the point where it would be best for us to travel non-stop in our wolf forms for safety and to give them warning. I'm also shocked we haven't come across a messenger yet."

"I was just thinking that," Themis says with a crease in his brow. "My guess is we'll come across one in the next two days. If we don't see one tomorrow, I might go in search of one.

I don't want to come on the main territory without giving warning."

"Why not?" Charlie pipes up, confused.

"We don't like when strange Lycans come into the main part of our territory," Zoya reports blandly. "Some of the Alphas in charge may take it as a bid for power or even an attack. It's better if we announce ourselves. And get the message to them as soon as possible."

The next day, a messenger crosses their path and Themis gives her the information of their intent to enter the northern territory in the next few days. After she is sent on her way, Themis indicates they should shift into their wolf forms. All in the party do as instructed and the five of them continue at a light trot as large wolves.

After only about a week and a half of travel, the group crests a hill, a sprawling expanse of what can only be described as a city spans out before them. In the area between them and the entrance to the city, forms rush in and out.

"*You ready?*" Themis asks in his low growl, looking between Cleo, Charlie, and Abrahm. "*You are about to see more Lycans in one area than you've seen anywhere.*"

Cleo sets her shoulders and gives a determined huff. "*Let's go.*" She gives herself a shake and begins to walk forward. Themis matches her stride on her right side. Zoya falls to her place to Themis's right while Abrahm and Charlie fall behind Cleo. All five of them as ready as they can be to face what will come next.

TO BE CONTINUED...

ACKNOWLEDGEMENTS

There are far more people to thank for helping me get this book out of my head and into the hands of those reading it than I think I have pages for, but I am certainly going to try.

First, I would like to thank my former creative writing teacher from Mayfield High School, Mrs.Kari Beery for first introducing me to the idea of National Novel Writing Month. You helped me start a yearly tradition that enabled me to get this book to a place where I felt comfortable to push it forward into the hands of an editor.

Next, a thank you to Briar Givens, who, despite our intermittent fallings in and out of communication over the years, has always encouraged me to write. Even if some of the ideas I wrote were a little on the outlandish side.

James Harris, I cannot thank you enough for connecting me with your own editor! Without you and your occasional nudges to try and get the book published, I'm not sure if this book would even exist in this form today.

Speaking of the editor, Alice Osborn, thank you for being such a wonderful editor. You helped me bring my 50,000 word mess of a novella into a full, publication worthy novel. I greatly appreciate the time and effort you put into helping me get the book to where it needed to be, and for occasionally checking in to see if I had reached out to any published yet.

Of course, I want to thank my parents for being supportive and encouraging of my writing hobby through the years, even though I often didn't let you read much of what I wrote. I thank you for all the books you bought me through the years that allowed me to learn how writing is supposed to be, and for always being a bit of a level head when it came to more "real world" stuff around the final processes of publication.

A final thank you goes to my husband Greg, who has stood with me these last 5 years and more as this book has gone from a fresh first draft written in 30 days, to a fully published book. Your support and encouragement has meant the world to **me**.

Made in the USA
Columbia, SC
10 May 2024

35111335R00148